Empty
Bottle
of
Smoke

by

Conon Parks

Book and Cover Design:
Vladimir Verano, Third Place Press

Cover Image Credits:

Original image: ⓒ 2016 'WTO Seattle,' Steve Kaiser via Flickr.com
Used under Creative Commons License v4.0

Author contact: antibes47@icloud.com

ISBN: 978-0-9975163-0-2

Printed at Third Place Press, Lake Forest Park, WA
on the Espresso Book Machine v.2.2.
www.thirdplacepress.com

In the beginning
there was nothing.
A rather difficult
scene to make,
if you dig

~Richard Farina

Based

upon

a

true

story ...

Chapter One

Liquid or Powder

Walter woke up believing he was buried under alluvial mud. Ah, but he was home! It was only an unpleasant dream. He fobbed about thru the covers, tangled and twisted — shuddering against the cold and cliché… thinking… what was it? Damn! He forgot to forget. He scratches himself — wondering what is really going on, realizing he is too young for prostate cancer. Where's his damn glasses? Stumbling over towards the refrigerator he opens it with squinty eyes taking out a carton of orange juice. Vitamin C is good for you… Hewie, Dewie and Lewie are all drinking it; it's all just ducks, Walter observes so diligently. The brightness of the red carton hurts Walter's pale eyes. He quits reading the back of the container. Walter drinks with gusto, tossing the empty colorful container into the waste basket, wiping his forearm across his lips, "Love only lesbians," he stutters out loud recalling the conversation he shared the night before with Danger Woman and her pals. They all seemed like nice dykes as his mind prances amid the dewy wild flowers. He rummages through the junk mail, advertising, coupons and religious monetary requests left on the television. He could get a free windshield with the purchase of a window thermometer with a money back guarantee on which you may return your purchase at any time f799or a full refund — but your sweepstakes prize is yours to keep! And dates with Ed McMahon and Dick Clark, the Australian Lottery for six million along with strategic prayer for Russia — Yes! I want to proclaim Jesus Christ to the people of the Soviet Union! (Make your check or money order payable to the Slavic Gospel Association of Wheaton, Illinois). Do you want to win the Lottery Now? Open envelope.

Walter opens the envelope. The head of some glib fat guy is pictured next to a caption in large bold print: "This guy is nuts! (and the in smaller print it reads) he's figured out how to pick Winning Lottery Numbers 93% of the time. Rather than just play the lottery himself — he's telling people about this. So far more than 500 people he's told have won — millions of dollars etc… etc… with instructions on how to sign up and how much money to send. More free information: $1000 FORFEITURE could happen for Failure to Claim your cash prize. Over the past year $10,000 cash winners did not claim their cash prize and therefore forfeited their $10,000 awards. Dang them Walter thought, fantasizing about what he would do with all that money. This looks like an interesting one from the Department of Unclaimed Merchandise Vault Facilities of Wuthering Heights Fine Jewelers, Canton Ohio. Walter tears it open. It reads: I hope I am writing the right person. Are you the Occupant that lives at 4127 Aurora Ave North? If in fact you are that same Occupant that lives at 4127 Aurora Ave N you are hereby notified that you will receive unclaimed merchandise etc… etc… "Lies!" Walter shouts…

Hmmm this looks rather interesting — a sexually oriented ad. This seems familiar for some reason. Walter reads more that is upon the envelope: Caution: the enclosed scientific data contains explicit medical references concerning human sexuality and male function. Do not open if you are under 21 or offended by graphic references of turgid biological functions. Secret Report of Soviet Doctors

Discovered. Boy this sure rings a bell, Walter tries to recall, but his short term memory is fuzzy. Walter opens up the envelope and out falls the photos of women primarily with their undergarments off in various states of action. It reads Top Secret. Top Secret is stamped all over them and "Actual Photos Reproduced from Smuggled Soviet Documents!" and in parentheses (We apologize for the quality of the photocopies but they are copied from the Russian document seized. All are authenticated by Military Intelligence U.S. Pentagon) Walter didn't think the photos were too bad — a little frolicking. It was further described as a "A Miracle Behind the Iron Curtain, an Elixer that turns the penis to Iron!" and then it went on with more data and history and information about impotent cosmonauts given a little West African Yohimbe bark could get it up with 43 Russian nurses that helped provide the necessary mental and physical stimulation to assist the test subjects — showing examples of how the Russians are willing to do anything for the good of "Mother Russia" with more photos, displays and examples. And then the order form for Top Secret Soviet Cosmonaut Formula that read: "Ya! Rush me the Top Secret Russki formula that has been smuggled out of Afghanistan by Freedom Fighters! It's about time we got some of the benefit out of the Soviets and this formula sounds like the Glasnost we need! Walter went and signed up his housemate for 40 units at $25. It was the minimum entry. He now recalled how it had worked quite well for a dear friend of his a few years ago. More stuff to read. How do they find him, Walter wondered? Not everybody receives this sort of mail. An official entry certificate so that one could have the guaranteed opportunity to win in a national give away; one just has to answer two $5,000 showcase questions, of course free gifts included. Showcase # 1 was a 7,000 sf fabulous luxury house of your dreams and showcase # 2 was an exciting vacation to Oahu Hawaii plus spending money. In each of them you get two choices to figure out the retail value of each price (they give you the numbers) and of course there are entry fees. Walter with Great Prosperity astutely surmised it was probably a scam. Yeah, Jimmy crack corn. Walter then picks up an anonymous looking letter and opens it up and reads from the plain typed black and white page:

I am a skeptical person by nature. I had received about 35 letters in about a 6 month period. However, there was something about this particular letter that I liked. The initial investment was a great deal less than any of the others, and I also liked the fact that all participants received money not just the person in the top position. Anyway, I sent out a 100 of these letters and hoped for the best. Everyday, I checked my mailbox hoping for a response. Nothing happened for the first 11 days, but on the 12th day, I received $137 in the mail. I couldn't wait until the next day. On the 13th day I received $383. On the 14th day I received $456 and on the 15th day I received $909. Over the next 4 1/2 months I received $131,000 in the mail. You wouldn't believe unless you try it... Sounds like a good deal and tax-free!

Walter goes on to read further instructions to the inner workings of the old chain letter Ponzi scheme... Silly chain letters, he allows it to float down upon the mauve shag carpeting. Ah, let's see what else has the U.S. Postal Service has so generously bestowed upon thee? A letter actually addressed to him. From Arkansas? Walter thought, "I don't like getting letters from Arkansas — there's not a lot of supervision in those states." Walter couldn't think of anyone he knew from Arkansas and had never set foot in Arkansas before but had heard enough strange tales and bizarre accounts of the Ozarks and of secret airfields with planes laden with confiture and cattle futures from Central America and the like — only rumors of course, but with all that the letter from Mena, Arkansas sent a shiver up his spine... of trepidation. As he opened the letter the goose bumps tingled up and down all the way down to his fruit of the looms.

The envelope is all wrinkled and smudgy with no return address. The scrawl was primitive — almost like chicken scratching. It started: Bet u never thought you'd hear from me again. Yep Annie git your gun! U think I just fell off the turnip truck, don't ya?

But I got my sources. We got a fence here too, keeps the neighbors from trespassin when they are out huntin bullfrogs, can't sik the dog on um: lib-er-als in conspire, black helicopters, the place has gone to piss, of course, in the old days we would just load up the shotgun with a little salt and popcorn, you ever seen a dog drunk? I bet u have... chasin their tail till they can't stand up straight — lots of drooling. Nowadays, if you give a dog just a nip, the law will get you for dog abuse, happened to a buddy of mine and it kept him in deep shit for half a year and all he did was let the dog drink out of his cup; seen him do it — he would lap it up a big gulp, raise his head up about to howl, but all that would come up was a gurgle, the dog ended up in the pound... ain't that somethink?

I'm comin up there to the Great Northwest to visit you Walter Annie and get matters ironed out between you and me once and for all.

U know who — The Apex Predator

"It's Louis Willy! I've got to move!... he must have escaped and found me out and he's always blamed me!... Oh my gawd!" and then Walter suffers a secondary vexation with the realization that for some inexplicable reason Louis continues to refer to Walter as Annie.

Walter is aghast and beside himself, he hastily picks up the letter from Andre, more like a small package: Morocco. It is from the Hotel Munria to be exact, ah yes — home of the Gene Genie! that's just like Andre — there's no sense in getting caught up in senseless factuality — as Jimi Hendrix plays his guitar on the beach in Essaouira — maybe... Well, it couldn't be any worse than this letter from the escapee in Arkansas, back with his kinfolk. And he's thrown in a paperback novel — a science-fiction western romance. Untitled.

Dearest Walter,

I'm shuffling the cards over an empty bottle of ouzo and candle light — contemplating a long one night stand...

"From the enslaved people came songs, chants and demands, while Princess and the Ruler are captive in prisons. In the future — they will be seen as headless, through idiots by holy prayers to heaven." Nostradamus wrote that Walter — hundreds of years ago and I think it makes sense as I sit here shuffling the cards right now over an empty bottle of ouzo and candle light — contemplating a long one night stand. To all my wealthy friends — all apologies... well, here it is with only a few touches missing — (got to get a title) but I felt obliged to dash off to you the proto-type, the model, it... being done and finally vanquished from the foamy cobwebs of a fuzzy past twisted into a fantastic tale, fantastic being defined more as absurd literature of fantasy etc... if you never want to speak with me again — I graciously understand. I hope everything is well with you as I continue my Re-search and work out the last lurid details of this science-fiction western romance. Walter — I want you to work as my agent. You will get a handsome cut from the future proceeds, but, of course. Give all my love to Señor Agape... that man is very dear to me.

Sincerely,

Andre

"That man is very dear to me?... give all my love? What the hell?... I think I'm missing something... once again." Walter crumples up the letter and dashes it into a corner as he exasperatingly pleads to the sheet-rocked painted walls, "My life is in danger and this dandy wishes all is well with me as he frolics on the Med continuing his ethnic Re-search in matters of love, he doesn't fool me as he's gently slipping into mental illness — I implore the gods! (a pause) life is not fair!... I've got to move... I'm being stalked like a little rabbit. I've got to think! I've got to move, where?... got to get away... get a hold of the Manifesto Party — they can hide me out, they will take care of me, help me, hole me up. It's a big place — help me... and it's free guns and dope for life!" Walter frantically begins to pack his belongings, scribbling an apologetic note to his young clerk apartment mate — recalling what his old sensei would always say — he who runs away, gets to fight another day... Remembering this was reassuring to Walter's panicked nerves as he composed his notice to vacate: "Dear Todd, did you say liquid or powder? — detergent — I mean. I got powder. As I've told you Todd in my work for the government — sometimes things come up. Vital things, national security issues — Homeland/der Fatherland matters of life and death. I'm not sure if I'm on the right boat and I'm not getting much response... Todd, the KGB and the Michoacán Cartel are hot on my trail and I'm not getting much response from my handlers — do you understand me Todd? am I making myself clear? Maybe I'll go back to reading and writing about agrarian reform in Latin America... and then we could all live happily ever after on rice and beans and plantains. What I'm trying to tell you Todd is I've got to go on the lam — government work... to protect our way of living — for the price of liberty is eternal vigilance. I hope it was powder. I mean detergent. Eat the message Todd as soon as soon as you've read and digested it. Maybe some day we'll all be together again. All I ever wanted was sunshine on my head. I have to leave now.

Walt

And with black motorcycle jacket, but no motorcycle he staged right... exiting the apartment door, Sir Walter With His Belongings, leaving the key, vacating his little white poverty zone with mingy sums of money, catching the short bus, to faithfully rely upon the kindness of strangers.

The behemoth of a building loomed like a gray tomb... a terrible beauty. The street of the hoi polloi was virtually deserted except for a few beat cars, some brothers playin dice — playin for cigarettes "Man thatsa six! thatsa six! One sez to Walter, "Hey funk-soul brother, what u doin uptown?" And the others go... "Doot da-doot — U-Bee, Wha-Bee, We-Bee, U-Pac, Tu-Pac, We-Pac..." Walter realizes perhaps he needs to work on his Ebonics and Esperanto; and there's a barefoot lady with a cigarette listlessly hanging, talking to herself, dragging a grocery cart filled with a black plastic garbage sacks, her belongings — puzzled and derelict; as the Indian, John T, who carves the red cedar, gazes peacefully as witness cuz he has seen it all and sees his death. It was a vintage Seattle Sunday morning, lead-gray sky, coming down. Broken 40 oz. malt liquor bottles strewn the grimy concrete sidewalk with old cigarette butts and a few dirty old weeds pushing up thru the cracks.

The weather was overcast and cheerless as Walter sauntered down the hill to ring the bell in front of the large doors to the loading dock hoping somebody would answer. Inside a guy who could use a shave groggily gets up from his deep slumber amongst a tangled web of woolen blankets, wooden pallets, and aluminum beer cans. First thing he does is cough and lights up a smoke. Amidst these environs everything is black, white and paler shades of gray, the dude wears a wife-beater and camies. As he sits there smoking the cigarette he ponders the night before, the day ahead, the years gone by and the various shapes of gray around him. He gets up to go to the toilet. "Must have gotten into one helluva fight last night: I think I might have broken my jaw..." There is a bell ringing but it's not in his head. The ringing continues. The guy goes about his business taking a long steamy pee — taking a look at the mirror five feet to the right of him staring at his tattoo. It's a tattoo from a place a long time ago. He wonders if he should get it transformed into something different, something interesting, something to forget just U.S.M.C. Maybe a colorful cockatoo. He shakes himself and turns so he's right square in front of the mirror taking a long hard look at himself below the anonymous florescent lighting, glaring into the mirror like in a motionless trance — Concentration, Focus — then... Ka-Boom! as the dude whips out a 9mm Beretta from behind his back and blows the mirror away. The look of bewilderment and utter horror that runs across the shootist's face belies that he didn't really mean to waste that mirror. "Shit! I thought I grabbed the empty clip! Gawd! First day on the job!" Taking the clip out he saunters out of the bathroom, grabs another smoke, hears the other ringing and yells, "WhAh-Aht!" He ambles his way across the subterranean space like a pinball attempting not to trip on any of the dark mounds and gray shapes. He peers out, eyeing a desultory dweeb in a Little Abner suit, funny-looking in a harmless way, kind of lumpy, sitting on his hapless haunches. It is Walter who has just had the last of his cigarettes absconded off by a group of kids — young toughs, unmonitored roisterers, bandying about with hockey sticks, but no skates — rude boys. A little song about them comes to Walter's head and he sings it — "take the skinheads bowling, take them bowling..."

"Who the fuk are you?! And what do you want?!"

"I'm Walter... I'm looking for Mister Maurice — you must be the new guy... the night-watchman."

The door opens. Walter is greeted by a stocky man of a Mongol cast.

"Yeah that's me, the keeper of the keys of the House of the Lord — Maintenance Supervisor... part of the survey team. Hey, you're not the asshole who called earlier to sell me aluminum siding and exercise equipment now are you?"

Walter, the refugee, shakes his head aggressively in denial. And then like an apparition the barefoot gibbering lady who was smoking a cigarette appears from behind and shouts at the night-watchman, "Sailor! I will walk 10,000 miles to weep upon your grave! If you wade in the water, it will drown you! Don't ignore what I say or it'll be your ruin! You will vanish like smoke leaving nothing but cold air behind you! Your glorious deeds do not warm us."

"Yeah go away now — Wouldja?!"

The beldam slithers off down the bleak street with her mumbo-jumbo Santeria voodoo and an occasional hackle-raising laugh. Her name is Cassandra.

"Who is that?" inquired Walter so innocently and open-eyed.

"That's my mom — who the fuk do you think it is? I don't know — Come on in."

"Anybody around?"

"Nope, just me and the rats."

"You gotta name?"

"You gotta warrant," the dude bristles back.

Walter sheepishly ambles around with an earnest attempt at admiring the fine arts ensconced in this bunker of a building graced under the banner name of the New Museum of Indecision and Hysteria and the We B Art Gallery. The night-watchman heads toward the back. Walter relaxes a bit — viewing the beautiful and the grotesque; paintings and large abstract metal sculpture, a wooden boat 15 or so feet long put together like a mini-pirate ship (the parrots looked good on it), graffiti on the red walls and black ceilings, modified trucks and motorcycles in the garage/loading bay, black and white photography of street scenes, a sign reads: Welcome to the Manifesto Party — Free Guns and Dope for Life! — comic books are strewn all around on a table along with revolutionary periodicals, union stuff, Indian rights, grape picker's rights, post-modern critiques and the preamble and constitution of the Manifesto Party: Doctrine and Dogma. All interesting material — (especially if you're crazy) The list of some of these fine publications included: The Militant, The Mao-ist Sojourner, The National Enquirer, Mad magazine, The Catholic Worker, The Revolutionary Worker, The IWW's Industrial Worker, The Worker's Worker, West Coast Sailor's Bulletin, Earth First!, The Star etc… etc… and a slew of others. In a graffiti-like scrawl written on a large wall is:

Dada postcards...

full of fugacity

amongst sartorial acolytes

filled with frenzied idealism

disrupting public tranquility

in middle class districts

running past the ruins

an epidemic of mental diseases

suffering from a poverty of passion

shouting out,   "God is Dead!"

What about the baby?!

Doesn't translate...

Walter's eyes scan more of the premises... seems there is some kind of religious shrine in the far corner with statuary of saints and pictures of the popes and Mary and Baby Jesus. A banner hangs in another corner and on it is written: Keep your distance in sword fighting and paintings. Colorful, but faded Buddhist flags hang limply over some steel shelving racks full of toasters and alternators. An old YMCA Zinsco Roll-O-Matic canvas-strapped, belly-shaking, fat-burning, jiggling, vibrating machine resolutely sits idle in the middle of an aisle. A red flag with a large black A for Anarchy is draped over a soft round comfortable beat sofa next to an old classic pinball machine. The head of a large animal hangs from a wall. To one side is a 3' x 3' photograph of John F. Kennedy shaking hands with some old cigar-smoking men in suits who looked like gangsters, or contractors — probably somebody's grandfather. A half shelled-out Willys station wagon lies forlornly in a lower garage/loading dock bay upon jack stands and behind it lies great wooden medieval-like doors used to keep the Saxons out.

Upon the garage walls painted in black in a large primitive hieroglyphics text against the gray din is written: Happiness is not based on one's self, it does not consist of a small home of taking and getting. Happiness is taking part in the struggle, where there is no borderline between one's personal world and the world in general...

Lee Harvey Oswald

Mesmerized, Walter repeated the words aloud like in a trance then he felt a dull jab in his back which caused him to jump nearly out of his skin and utter a feeble yelp of "Yikes!" only to hear a sinister, guttural pronouncement from behind him, "If I was VC — you'd be dead... like some coffee? cream or sugar? liquid or powder?" as the new night-watchman judiciously bestows upon Walter a large tin cup full of piping hot black coffee.

"Make yourself at home. I'm Mac," extending his callused paw outward. Could use a little Vaseline intensive care upon those mitts Walter thought. Maybe some bag balm. He also noticed that on Mac's left fist upon the four knuckles was tattooed MARY.

"I guess we're not open till 2:00, that's when Brother Maurice comes in to open and hang the mirrors and I go to my other job. Was there anything else that you might require? I thought I'd make me some grits."

Mac sure smokes a lot. Walter looks down and mutters nearly inaudibly, "Uh…no… uh-umm was wondering if maybe I mean I could help out here, mop and clean, I'm a good typist and if maybe, I know there is a lot of room and was wondering if maybe I could stay here for a while. I've got a job and could pay some rent because you see there is this crazy guy after me."

Mac waits and ponders surmising the situation; staring blankly at Walter up and down and then… snaps! "It's up to the Committee; but fortunately for you the manager is away on a freighter haulin fish-meal to Russia for the next month or two, workin as a wiper — he's crazier than a shit-house full of bats. I'm just the night-watchman. (Mac immediately realizes a plan that he'll just pocket the extra potatoes for rent from Walter as well as get him to do a lot of Mac's work detail — Oh yes… Indeed…) Mac goes on, "You probably wouldn't like it if he was here — least that's what everybody tells me, but… it's cool with me, got a nice couch over there by the pool table… But! It's up to the Committee. Could be the Vigilance Committee or the Committee of Public Safety."

Mac grabs a handy spray can of Black Flag and starts amply squirting the floor. "Party's over! Gads! The roaches are terrible here, worse than my last place. So some crazy guy is after you? And the cattle all have got brucellosis and your wife has shot your horse and peed on the carpet. That's really too bad… probably can't even get a date to prom, what'd you say your name was?"

"Walter."

"Yes! Walter… Walter Without Belongings, I see… that's really too bad. Damn bugs!" as Mac carries on strategically spraying the Black Flag in certain nooks and crannies as Walter struggles to keep stride with Mac. A little classical music plays in the background. The phone rings. Mac stops spraying and heads across to answer. Walter tells him he's got to go to the bathroom.

Mac points. "Head's that way — don't mind the chamber pot." Realizing as he says it that Walter already knows where the boudoir is in this dimly lit warehouse full of dubious collectibles — art, just call it art. The phone keeps ringing as Walter pushes open the bathroom door immediately noticing the shattered mirror. He examines it all closely, getting the faint whiff of cordite. Walter goes into denial and takes a leak, shuddering at the sight of a past visitation left as a little floating territorial reminder in the toilet bowl to only befoul the sensibilities of the next patron of the commode. Flushes, washes his hands and elects to remain in denial while reading parts of the Dr. Bronner's 18 in 1 pure peppermint castile soap bottle about Jesus, Mohammad, Karl Marx, Mark Spitz and Hamlet getting his moral ABCs for We're All-One of All-One God Faith. We're All-One! All-One! All-One! good stuff, good soap, the old rabbi produced; and good for the wee-wah too, get you humming right around there — definitely magic soap... Walter re-reads it, but then he can't help but overhearing Mac on the phone shouting into it:

"The conservatives are fools!... Kaczynski's right and so was Alinsky, yeah, yeah... No! The Revolution must be a school of unfettered thought! Optimism is about sheer terror! You are obfuscating the issue, buck up man! Woodstock was fucking stupid... What kind of Maoist are you anyway? I know... I know... I know the War on Drugs is just the War upon the Peasants. Change must come thru the barrel of a gun... Come comrade... in the spirit of Christian reconciliation... Viva Zapata! Yeah back in Havana... Indeed. It was an epidemic that hit the beach and killed off most of the art colony: cirrhosis of the liver... Uh-huh... Ok... The assassination bureau... Ummm... yes, I do think that Baader-Mienhoff had a point. Uh-huh. Send lawyers, guns and money. But the Sandinistas are simple campesinos mi amigo. There are no Contras! They don't exist... there is only the CIA. The Contras are us! We are all Mafia! Yeah, yeah Noriega/Bush baby and the House of Saud... And what of the Red Brigade? Propaganda! But all we want is peace in northern Ireland... I understand that... Proletariats! Yes! Nooooo... Susan Sontag?! Absolutely.

"Yes, I understand that if it wasn't for the outstanding Marxist leadership of Thomas Sankara the African nation of Burkina Faso would still be Upper Volta or something... does it relate? Yes! it does relate... am I on the right boat? Who the hell am I talking to anyway?! Hello?... Hello?... He hung up!" Mac explodes! Slams the phone down.

Quickly Mac regains his composure, realizing he is being watched, he implores sympathy from a puzzled, slightly alarmed Walter who is now standing before him. At least, his eavesdropping on the curious telephone exchange allowed him to temporarily forget the dramatic demise of the bathroom mirror.

"Who was that?"

"That was my stockbroker — he's a sick man."

Mac opens one of the old refrigerators and grabs a beer. He is sweating profusely. The artificial light of the refrigerator resembles a beacon in the gray shrouded atmosphere. On its antiquated rounded yellowy white door is written: Attencion chien bizarre! Mac pounds down the beer — a Grain Belt/Rhinelander. Mac asks Walter if he'd like one.

"We've got pallets of this stuff downstairs in the root cellar — compliments of the Brothers Longshore of ILWU — an injury to one is an injury to all — you ever been down there? Part of old Underground Seattle, there's a whole city twenty feet below — it's unbelievable! Vampires, night-stalkers, Kolchak, purple glass, faro tables, opium dens and pallets of beer. A concrete jungle — like an abandoned slaughterhouse; it's the catacombs! — and you can get anywhere..." as he shakes one in front of Walter. Walter displays signs of resistance. Mac grabs another, opening it, drinking it more slowly as the froth oozes...

"What's wrong mate — life got you down? You don't want a Grain Belt/Rhinelander? How about a smoke out of this here clear glass peace pipe? Come on, give it the old college try."

Walter displays signs of anticipation but shakes his head cuz who knows what ol Mac may have in that little smoking utensil — Mexican black tar?

"Hesitation kills dude — maybe later?" as the little blacks of his eyes light up.

"Yeah it's a little early for me right now Mac — but thanks anyway," kind of sheepishly with a few hems and haws. "I think I'll watch some TV till Mr. Maurice arrives. Isn't there some kind of sports games on?"

"What do I look like Howard Cosell or something? Terry Bradshaw? Go over there — there's 5 or 6 TVs, black and white and colored, turn on all the channels, free cable! Maybe you can find a cricket match on one of them. I don't like cricket... I prefer jai alai — a Basque thing."

The atmosphere instantly seemed to become energized with a suspended feeling of anger and despair, a perfection in control as everything moved thru time. Mac brooded the prior jovial left just as quick as it came.

"What happened to the mirror in the bathroom?"

"I shot it."

"Oh..."

"Any more questions?"

"No..." Walter stammered as he nervously flitted thru the pages of some skin magazine. Mac finished off his beer and attended to custodial duties — searching for contraband, as he put it. Walter had to admit to himself he did enjoy looking at pictures of naked female rodeo clowns. They were pretty and laughing. Then he had to stop. He was having un-natural thoughts; so he closed his eyes and all because he thought he might go blind, turn to stone, or become like a salt sculpture, good heavens! maybe even start interfering with himself or something... who knows and then a thought came across him and it made him wonder — where was the cheese in his hamburger? Mac then came back swinging some Arnis Filipino fighting sticks in a casual Bruce Lee bad mojo-way.

"Ah I see you have come upon an exhibit from the private art collection of the vacant manager who is now bobbing around, somewhere out in the North Pacific — losing even more fragments of his already fractured and shattered feeble mind... gently slipping into mental illness… So Walter, some crazy guy is after you, huh? So Walter and… you're wondering what to do next?"

Walter's own enfeebled mind careens — did he just call me Annie?

"What's your next move? What's your next step? Coming here was probably a good first thing to do…" as Mac keeps on extrapolating as well as twirling the nasty wooden sticks of menace — doin that wu-tang thing,

"Yes Walter — as it is said, be swift as thunder that peals before you have a chance to cover your ears, fast as the lightning that flashes before you can blink your eyes. Sun Tzu — The Art of War… as it is said."

Walter just stood there blinking, disbelieving — as Mac just rambles on.

"ALWAYS solve the problem that is going to kill you first… yeah you know — we are just not in control. Control is an illusion. Do you have any control over the crazy man who wants you dead? No. He's just been sicced on you from God High Above — Life! man and there ain't a damn thing you can do about it — and from that you can come to realize that you are not that important — you might be special Ed, but you are not special (Mac puts a funny dripping with sarcasm emphasis on the word "special") with no special rights and it is basically because nobody gets out of here alive — we are all going to die. You are going to die Walter! When?! You don't when, how?… nuthin! just one day, you'll die and they'll lower you down six feet in a moldering wooden box… cuz it's not about you! You just got to know one thing and just one thing good. Life is hard man, life is hard, and that's why it is so cool to survive man, can you dig it! U gots to get up real close to smell the enemy. Get in Condition Yellow always wary like a dog ready to fuck, fight or flight. You think the panther in the wild has angst and worries about all this existentialist shit?" Mac laid down his nasty stick and finished his last statement with a final chug of gusto off the old can of animal beer. His eyes had come alive and were very black with twinkling, burning-like little stones of onyx and fire opal. He does a few leg stretches and saunters over to the body bags to deliver a couple of wicked round-house kicks and as he works out kicking and punching away, delivering blow after blow, doin more of that wu-tang thing, he shouts at Walter with ferocious anger and power: "always carry violence in your back-pocket," bam! bam! ptow! ptow! as the bag seems to explode with the jangling of the chain, "seeking..." pow! "perfection in control... always know," bam, bam, kthud! "always remember that Nothing is assured... most people are illogical," blam, ptow... "non-rational; most of us are prejudiced and biased, blighted with emotional garbage and preconceived notions with jealousy, suspicion, fear, ignorance, envy and pride," kpow! thud "and what you really need to remember Walt is most folks don't want to change their minds..." blam, kpow!... "bout their religion, their girlfriend, or their barber, communism or Nirvana... 'if we are all thinking the same — then somebody's not thinking' — Patton, General George Patton." slam! kabam! pow! "got it! get it! And pay attention to what you read from the fortune cookies."

Extremely winded Mac stops, "Shit... whew, gettin old... and remember man," taking a swoop off a beer, "all art is useless..." Walter takes note of the sweaty lather Mac has worked himself into. Mac ambles over to another nearby old decrepit refrigerator and reclaims another can of cold beer, lighting up, taking a drag, looking out the large murky bay windows out across at the gray buildings and the gray clouds as the rain fell on the empty streets as everything moved thru time. Walter contemplates 24 hours in a day, 24 beers in a case — coincidence? Two of the TVs are on — they are nature programs; one is of a cheetah running down a young wildebeest, the other is of a lion protecting her kill of a zebra from a pack of hyenas. Nature is rough thinks Walter. Mac goes on talking to himself, reminding himself, reiterating to himself as he spoke to Walter as if in soliloquy: "There's a hidden principle... the individual must disappear — that we are nothing is not the same as we are small... Is that It? And you do the hokey/pokey, and you turn yourself about... and that's what it's all about. Ye-ah. They keep telling us — We are nothing! The individual must disappear. It is a state of war... set loose upon the land... you know and life becomes like a movie as you look back, looking forward and all that rage and humiliation come together in one and you put it down and nobody is listening and you've got to sit back in some dirty movie parlour eating popcorn all by yourself again and again until all the rage and humiliation come together in one and you put it down and hope someone is listening, damnit…" Mac pauses, "how temporal life is… Remember! Rules for Conduct: Don't count on anyone, accept no gifts, buy nothing in the presence of others, say as little as possible, ask for nothing, don't waste time defending your opinions, remain autonomous and alone. You gots to have guts, focus, strength, smarts, righteousness, ruthlessness and luck!"

The phone suddenly rings. A Siamese cat leaps upon Walter's head, knocking off his coke-bottle thick glasses. He shrieks — "I can't see! I can't see!"

Mac shouts, "Ah Godot likes doing that to visitants and future friends," as the baboon of a cat stealthily scurries off into some detritus-filled nook and a parrot flies around screeching: "pecker-pecker, pecker-pecker." And Walter is reminded of when he was a kid and going to that gray-green institutional sealing wax stinky awful old-folks home and visiting an ancient merchant seaman/mariner great uncle of his named Thor, who mostly stood in a corner drooling in his bed shirt saying: "pecker-pecker… pecker-pecker," to himself. It made Walter cringe. "Polly wants a cracker…" snipes Mac.

Mac gets to the phone and all Walter hears is: "Which way did they go?!… How many were there?! How fast were they going?!… I must find them. I am their leader." Click. He hung up.

"Who is this guy?" Walter says, thinking aloud, "What is this place?" He'd only visited the gallery/Manifesto World Headquarters a couple of times (once for a friendly game of craps) prior to having just recently moved to Seattle from Portland five months ago and getting the temp job at the Trendsetter Corporations Collections department which had been demanding a brutal amount of his precious time; a lot of people just couldn't afford all that exercise equipment, vinyl windows and aluminum siding. Five months out of Portland and already Louis Willy is on to me. It must be a spy! Where's Señor

Agape? Where in the hell in India could he be? And who is this Mr. Maurice guy, a man of such impeccable taste and culture — shared a few words of the French vernacular with him at the Cafe Viaggio and voila! here I am — claims to know Señor Agape from the Days of Rage, the Situationist years back in Paris, San Francisco and Chicago. Could be? Thinking, thinking aloud like twister in the sun; all this socialist noir, the process continued as Walter's mind worked in amazingly episodic, inconsistent, dizzying, heightened, paranoid fashion. It was too big; his brain that is. Sometimes it even made his head wobble to one side or the other. A doctor had prescribed some muscle-building neck exercises for Walter, but it was all too athletic.

Mr. Maurice, Señor Agape, Andre, Danger Woman, Louis Willy, Didier, the Brothers Berrigan, Baby Nambu and now this Mac character. What did Life have in Storage for him now? All he had ever wanted was sunshine on his head. A nice peaceful life with some kind of chubby bookish myopic woman that would come by occasionally, darn his socks and feed him his pudding. Yes, yes — yes, that was it! Man needs a maid! He had applied to the U.S. Postal Service, seeking glorious conformity, but then all the in-house shootings swept across the fruited plain of this great nation's mail centers as disgruntled employees took it out on their ill-fated co-workers. So he went to work at McDonald's as an assistant manager trainee and then it started happening in those fine restaurants across the republic — mayhem and melee — maniacs with guns taking it out on all the bovine eaters — it just wasn't fair. For the cows or the people. Feeling like the organ player for Dylan when he went electric and the folkies went nuts; Walter simply quit in fear for his life and now was just a temp for various collection agencies. Good job security. Maybe he should just sell advertising to fulfill the secular prayers of the American public like his Uncle Ed. Anyway, back to this Manifesto Party business… Again, Mr. Maurice, a guy he met and exchanged a few words of French with at the Viaggio Coffee Shop, off Prefontaine, just tucked in there under the hill, and since then has been actively recruiting him for months… for what? It made the monkey fur on his head curl just thinking about it. Suddenly shaken from his internal dialogue.

"Hey do you have a driver's license, dude? I got to get to my other job and the bus is just so slow…" Walter surmised the implicit demand and requirement in the seemingly innocuous inquiry.

As per agreed upon Mac's behest, Walter assumed the position in the driver's seat. "This is really cool, man." Mac said with alacrity as he jumped into the passenger's seat. It was a green Ambassador circa early 1960s. Kind of that hunter kelly green color from the Green Hornet TV show — very funky, very stylin. On the back was two bumper stickers — one read: Official Exhibit of the New Museum of Hysteria and Indecision. in plain back and white, Oriental-like text and the other read: "Freedom for Chinese Jews." Wasn't exactly the kind of automobile one would expect to see a chap like Mac cruising in. But what kind of automobile would one expect to see Mac in? A GTO thought Walter. Or an old Camaro. Some kind of muscle. But the Ambassador hauled ass with a 351 Windsor. Or was it a 454? Walter didn't know.

"What about Mr. Maurice?"

"Ah, he'll be here soon enough to open, paint the ceiling black, cows of France…" Walter presumed his hearing was slipping since first encountering Mac. It must be the psilocybin still between his ears.

"Ah yes, Mister Maurice — soon we'll have to cure him of his dirty French habits."

"So where are we going?"

"Ah, we're going to work."

"Well, where is it?"

"It's all around… I move around a lot in my work."

"Well what direction should I go?" with slight impatience.

"Go this way," and he pointed straight ahead, "I will give you the directions. Jesus Made Seattle Under Pressure — Go to James, take Madison, up to Seneca, down Union, over to Pike."

"What is your job anyway Mac, if you don't mind me asking?"

"I am a representative for a company. The Interarms Corrections Corporation of America — more crime equals more prisons equals more business. I work with the Public Disorder Intelligence Division. They hired me out of Lompoc — had to do a couple of years… it's all part of our rigged economy." Mac says as he straightens the tilt of his Billy Jack hat.

Well, that was just about enough question and answer time for Walter. He just decided to drive and go get a hamburger or something. So as they drove it appeared to Walter that they were taking a most circuitous route. They wound up driving by the gallery in seven or eight various loops around the city. Constantly looking into the rear view mirror, Mac's focus in scanning the streets was extraordinary to Walter. There never was any mention amongst the dynamic duo that they kept on returning whence they begun — to this place of origin — as the police scanner squawks…

"Ok, ok, ok we're clear! Go, go this way now — a couple of klicks," Mac points, "On to the Catholic Seaman's Club! I've got a friend there — I need to pick up something; then we head over to the Sailor's Union of the Pacific. Gits some vigorish. A little shakedown. And then on to Lacey-O'Malley Bail Bonds."

Clear of what? I guess nobody is tailing us Walter presumed starting to wonder if maybe he should have just checked into the YMCA. The car wheels hiss against the pavement into the super unknown.

All keyed up on dope, just like Detroit Red aka Malcom X, Walter had been moving stuff at night with Mac for several consecutive evenings. It was near Halloween indeed. Ordnance ensued, never too sure of where, what and why and opting not to finding out the answer to many of his questions, feeling just a slight bit more solace and bliss in his ignorance, Mac volunteering very little; Walter asking fewer — only simple directions — like a passenger, but driving. High in that marijuana glow, where the world relaxes, Mac would be so calmly wired as they prowled about like rats in the dark under the street lit lights of the black night. They would load and unload boxes and bags and office equipment to and fro from the various locales to the Ambassador. Mac referred to it as confiture. Caches of guns occasionally as well. Or so it seemed. Plausible deniability maintained. Deals masked with a patina of legitimacy. Sometimes a black-haired, black-eyed, hawk-nosed Croat named Josef who had a couple of used car lots and chop shops on Aurora/Highway 99 and Lake City Way would be on the sorties, as well — though he had limits for the physical work due to the missing of his right foot. Mac and him would argue with words Walter could barely translate. Like they were speaking some sort of pidgin gypsy. Mac would call him Grinning Ustasha. And so many ouzos and cigarettes later, Josef would go on, "You know, my grandfather always said to me... if you are in the woods and you have one bullet and you run into a bear and a Turk — shoot the Turk... a ha-ha-ha... you know, stealing cars, it is so eazee; you never get caught... and Mac! — you know what the Jews did to Christ?!" All the moving was "business" related — Mac would insist, but of course, while hopelessly naive Walter very consistently remained terribly ignorant of contents and amounts. He at times would look over at Mac and say to him — "Hey que hombre — lower the bunduki" — you know, an M-1 carbine, an SKS, or a pistol-gripped 12 gauge pump shotgun. That's a little Swahili for gun that Walter learned from Mac... 'bunduki' — don't you know, gettin down with the Mau Mau... Back when Mac was in Nairobi for the coup of '82... where they picked up the shifta Kamau who had been runnin with the panga gangs.

"Oh sure, yeah," Mac would reply so reasonably and put the gun down enough so that the barrel would not at least be discernible from the street by a cart full of cops. But still always at ready as if — on patrol. Nothing like a gun to make you want to share...

Much smoke billowed forth out of the cab of the Ambassador on those frosty evenings. Bottles clinked as the CB channels were switched. It was at times amazing to Walter how so much of the time in his required assistance of Mac it had to be done under cover of darkness — loading and unloading. Kind of dawned on him once in a while as to just how weird it was sometimes.

Of course, Walter was mostly just helping Mac move his belongings from one domicile funky hotel, to a used car lot, to another large warehouse full with pallets stacked high of bottles of olive oil with

the name of that Italian outfit, the Valentinos, who owned the ships
from Western Pioneer that Walter and Mac sometimes longshored
for on the off-loads of crab, salmon and cod, (which to Walter —
working down there, was basically — Lord of the Flies — with very
many large men) and onto another coincidence and another abandoned warehouse to another used car lot or chop-shop of Josef's with
his assistants — Hey-soos and Ahn-hell (Jesus and Angel in Spanish
from La Ciudad de Dios, Durango — City of God — Mexico; Mac
had said so very casually it was a good place to get your head chopped
off and what nice names Josef's "helpers" had for a couple of thievin
hoods as Josef abusively shouted at them, "This ain't camp! This ain't
no piñata party! Do it professional! Not Mexi-Can!") and back to
the Hotel Morrison and over to the Hotel Panama to seemingly
deserted warehouses off Magnolia or the SODO or Harbor Island,
with tumbleweed ambling about to another no-tell motel to more
coincidences. It just happened Mac had a lot of belongings all over
the city of Seattle and they just all happened to be in various nooks
and crannies of madness and chaos with empty whiskey bottles. And
it is just weird sometimes, thought Walter, while out on patrol with
Mac. Just a little weird... And then Mac went on, "It's all about the
democratization of cocaine, don't you see? — crack — a little water,
a little Arm & Hammer baking soda, and a little heat, that's all you
need... start sellin cocaine with some procaine, set up a house, and
sell for $5 to $25 a pop. You just smoke it... and we end up sup-
porting the right political gunmen from Jamaica to Nicaragua with
a little help from Rev. Sun-Myung Moon's Unification Church...
and make beaucoup money... you see it's all a cash business and so
is selling used cars, plus we can store the cocaine in the trunks. It's
a dark alliance, I'm telling you too much... and then he muttered,
"You chose your path. We are stardust... musta washed my hands in
a muddy water... musta washed my hands in a dirty stream... I like
my bitterness shaken not stirred... as the poppies bloomed." and he
begins to sing: "and all the bells were ringing... and all the people
were singin... you can't raise a Caine back up when he's in defeat...
and all the people were singin na na na na na na na na na na na na na
na... You chose your path... you chose your path..." A coyote from

nowhere runs in front of them on the downtown streets and Mac says: "Think! This my Spirit — Untouched By Humans." And the coyote looks back at Mac and disappears into the red night.

South Park mini-mart; dumpy, depressed with hazy light and color from neon. People amble and float around. Desperate. Lost-like. They got troubles. There's a hardness...

"Hey pull over here to this mini-mart I want some smokes and zoo-zoos."

Walter obediently pulls over to the dank mini-mart. Waiting — nervous... poor people made him nervous... they're so unpre-dictable. There was some kind of picket line of about a dozen or so — with signs saying something about the Wobblies and Strike!

Mac gets back and says, "Go this way I gots to make a delivery," they go a few blocks down and, "hey pull over here — you stay in the car — these guys are kind of weird... keep the car going — don't shut it off. Pay attention. I'll be right back."

Moments later, Mac returns, his breath letting out a gust of steam against the cold air.

"Let's go," shaking his left hand a bit. "Had to do a little trimming. Let's go pick up an eight-ball." And off they went to friendly taverns where Mac would feed Walter with disco lemonade and smokes and then let him crash on one of the couches back at the Manifesto Party Headquarters.

On one of their sojourns as they were making their way to the friendly taverns like Spin's or Angie's or the Dome Mac inquires: "Ever noticed like what's with Seattle? Every carpenter or guy in the trades is either a gonnabe/wannabe guitar-playin rockstar or has got like a masters degree in philosophy or psychology? Like how about that dude on the docks over at Pio — got a degree in French from Yale? And how everybody's a fuckin hero in this country now? War-riors — we're a nation of warriors. Warriors and heroes. Thank you for your service... service... service... Nobody can just be a poor fucker who got blown up. You know — just some poor fuckin sap reserve private drivin a deuce truck that gets blown up hittin a im-provised explosive device, a booby-trap — basically, a mine — on the road to Damascus... I see no Glory. You know — Life. Yeah in Amerika — we are heroes because we watch TV. You ever done any bounty hunting Walter Annie? You ought to do somethin about that dandruff. Get you some Selsun Blue."

Walter's mind insisted that it heard no part of any of the questions just asked and instead he concentrates on his driving as he became hypnotized by the rhythm and back and forth of the windshield wipers as his head involuntarily wags back and forth, back and forth.

"It's all about love... it's all about love... no one knows the minute or the hour — you want a perfect church, don't join a church; you want a perfect union, don't join a union... it's all good... it's all good... it could be worse... it could be worse... and now you know what it's like... to sing the blues... aye you know where there's love there's Irish and where there's hate there's more Irish... no more peck o corn for me... my mother was born somewhere along the Yukon River... O Puff the Magic Dragon, lived by the sea... Puff was a two prop DC-3 turned gunship: military designation C-47 not to be confused with a CH-47 double-rotor helicopter. It had 30mm miniguns and then the spectre ships would come in, slowly circling, makin like one long burping sound, could cover every square inch of football fields just a rainin down metal; hate to be a gook with that shit comin down — Puff the Magic Dragon... Yeah, Fayette-Nam, we be pullin up to Ft. Bragg and there's a billboard there to greet you: Welcome to Fayetteville — Heart of the KKK — Home of Robert K. Shelton Grand Wizard Dragon or whatever and they got this guy on horseback in the KKK outfit, horse's got the sheets on too. What a world... Yeah, we are already dead... the End... Nam, Nam, Nam... Fayette-Nam, I want to live a life of danger! I want to be an Airborne Ranger!..." as Mac would slip into these reveries so many pops later from the usual quantity of ardent spirits he explains to Walter that as an "incorrigible youth" he'd been given the choice of jail or the Marines. He chose the later and DaNang at seventeen, finished his tour in-country with the Corps, was out for a few months, but just couldn't relate, "combat-oriented" they termed it; decided to join the Army and jump out of airplanes. Walter driving slowly thru the black of the night with the honk of the car horns contemplates his career opportunities with Trimsetter Corporation collections department, his political aspirations with the Manifesto Party, Leonard Nimoy's poetry and his inability to meet normal decent human beings unlike all his wealthy friends... but Walter didn't really have no wealthy friends; and he considers the possibility of a tryst with Danger Woman and maybe one or two of her friends — the imagination of the mind is limitless — she had affronted his usual dormant masculine sensitivities with the insistence that he was too delicate and fragile of constitution. Walter did harbor his own self-doubt, but no guts! no glory! Isn't that what they say? It hurt just making him think about it — what she might do. Mac, the deep drinker, snored loudly as Walter eased the hunter green Ambassador up to the no parking fire lane next to the New Museum of Hysteria and Indecision. All part of the American roulette druggie-drag ragtime U.S.A. Walter realizes there is still time to straighten out his life, but not a helluva lot. Over and Out.

Some nights later: Walter hears the rattling and scrambling through his shroud of dark dreams. He rolls to his less stiffened side on to the lumpy over-stuffed couch and through one eye espies the supper dish belonging to the old black dog that Mac keeps for "security purposes." The black dog is not making the infernal racket however and Walter's other eye pops open in horror as he beholds a large brown rat, Rattus Norvegicus, the dreaded Norway Ruf, new to Seattle's shore, taking a light lunch at the expense of the aforementioned black dog. He shudders at the thought that this creature is fit to survive in the most unforgiving of environments, will eat man's food and yea, the corpse of man himself if necessary. Walter's brains reels at the stock of unwanted information he has subconsciously collected over the years concerning this loathsome creature that can jump three and a half feet straight up from a stand still, a vector-bearing most vermin, transmitting diseases with impunity, the unbidden litany continues... Suddenly, a ruby glow bathes the feasting rodent and he hears a flat "splat!" as the rodent does a seemingly impossible forward flip and alights on its back; legs twitching, its head vanished somehow in the course of this arcane maneuver. He stares at the still convulsing corpus and hears a low throaty chuckle as

Mac silently steps out of the darkness, an apocalyptic vision in dark mottled black, gray and rifle-green coveralls. A black watch-cap is jammed down his head with a head-lamp emitting a focused beam of red light in any direction Mac happens to be looking at the moment.

"Hunh, hunh, hunh," he chuckles, "dining and dancing in the old town tonight." Walter is frozen in standard confusion as Mac steps up to the dish and tsk, tsk softly, "Shit, splattered She-Mutt's food with mousy brains. Not good, better toss it out." Walter watches as Mac empties the dog dish into a plastic sack and then picks up the now stilled rat corpse with a black-gloved hand, dropping it unceremoniously into the same sack. He turns to Walter smiling lasciviously, "yeah, little fuckers probably eat up ten bucs worth of dog food a month. I hate'em, that's why the dish stays out here, as bait don't you know?"

Walter's sleep is totally wasted by this moment and Mac's seemingly casual out-take on this little horror has snapped Walter's conscious to a tingling electrified state. Mac reaches into his copious cargo pockets and pulls out two cans of beer proffering one to the recumbent Walter who accepts out of sheer reflex. Mac pops his top and chugs heartily and sets down the can between black Red Ball Jet sneakers and lifts up a small black pistol with a disproportionately large barrel. Walter's eyes bulge in disbelief.

"You're hunting rats with firearms?! In the city?!"

Mac fiddles with the piece dropping the magazine and jacking the action with one practiced hand catching the ejected round on the fly and turning eyes hard as ice to Walter.

"Yeah, no shit, what of it?"

He casually answers as he inserts a loaded magazine. Walter's mind spins, "Oh my God, protect me in my time of need. Save me from armed lunatics and your own fundamentalist followers in their legions." Mac takes a long pull from his beer and taps the can's top with the sausage thick barrel of his little pistol.

"Yeah, buddy — Godot and the feral cats here can't do it all; and I know it's illegal to discharge firearms in the city limits, but I'm doing my civic duty ridding our fair streets of the filth and vermin that debases our community's exquisite sense of aesthetics and what is humanity… besides the way you get caught is by being heard doing it…" he pauses for effect.

"This here is your basic Berretta jetfire modelo 951 in .22 long with a threaded barrel which accepts a sound suppressor you can buy from the Gunlist Monthly by mail order as a dummy silencer." Walter has himself a drink to give himself time to digest this information.

"But if it's a dummy silencer?…" Mac holds up his black-gloved hand, "they also include instructions on how to construct a working model using the casing and fittings included; I just provide the steel wool and washers and perforated tubing for the innards. Pretty neat, huh?" He takes another pull from his beer and lights a Pall Mall with the flick of his Zippo lighter.

"Yeah that and I use CCI .22 CB caps, so it's essentially a subsonic round but within 50 feet it hits like a .22 long rifle, cool, huh?"

He gets up and walks off into the stygian darkness and says to Walter, "Remember this maxim, just because it didn't happen, doesn't make it any less real. Later, sweet dreams buddy. Careful what you get good at."

Walter finishes his beer and shudders involuntarily in the knowledge of dreams of headless rats dancing in his mind for the remainder of the night. And pillow-biting. As the barracks were made rhythmic by Mac's compulsive… snoring.

Cool, cruel world… city full of morgues. Kill the messenger…

Maurice kicks the few empty tallboy cans and 40 oz. bottles of malt liquor out of his way cursing under his breath — "Merde" — as he spits upon the pavement towards the street flicking the butt of his Gitane down upon the sidewalk. His alert Gallic eyes scan his surroundings warily; the street corners, the parking garage across the way and up towards the old yellowing apartment building looking down upon him. A large banner waves listlessly from one of the fourth floor windows — "God is a Giant Insect!" with a couple of other indiscernible messages splayed across some of the other windows.

Crazy people live in that building. Everybody needs a home. Maurice just wished it wasn't right across from the gallery — what with Kucera Gallery and Foster/White Art moving in, a brand new fire-station: the neighborhood was changing and that meant there is money to be made. But some change is slow and some things never change and there really is — nothing new under the sun. The milling bedraggled men line up and down at the mission filing in slowly one by one to attend the religious service for soup program. Up the street, in the park of the realm of hungry ghosts, some sisters shout out singing Gospel music from a crackling PA system to soothe the souls gathered about and sitting upon the park benches for the purpose of saving the spiritually bereft — a legion of the lost, cohorts of the damned, les undesirables — proof of an unshakable canard of America. Some brothers raptured in another dice game stage like a murder of crows. A guy in cammies and sporting a Mohawk shouts at the methadone shop to open up. Everything appears normal. Maurice, the sous officier, adjust his jaunty beret and takes out his key and enters the gallery turning on the lights, petting the large Siamese cat there to greet him so judiciously.

"Ah Godot, ça va? What have you to report to me today that has gone on lately herein this art asylum?" he speaks in a gruff French peasant accent. "Ah bon chat, good kit-tee… I hope Messieur Mac has been treating you well. No?! I will speak with him immediately about these matters. Ah, I don't feel so good myself… too much red… red wine last night at The Storeroom and that goddam Black Label of Joey Piss-drunk's! O Joe how could you treat me this way? hey hey…" As he recalls how Piss-drunk Joe with his Mohawk and Paul from RPA, always lookin like Sid Vicious, along with many others, had come up with this fusion of punk rock and garage band with the right drugs, to consummate the Seattle flannel marriage of what is now called grunge… O remnants of the night before… you broke my heart… the loud furious music of Crisis Party, the O so sweet recall before Bill the Sculptor decided to jump up on the table and rant on about Estonian Independence and pull down his pants. O the horror… the horror… it made his head hurt — 86'd from another fine establishment; but they all made it out alive… wound up down on the Kalakala — the floating toaster down on Lake Union, the old techno-deco ferry boat dragged down from Kodiak Island where it had suffered an ignominious fate as a cannery, where now Bill was the night-watchman — the steel hulk was full of ghosts at night. You could sometimes hear the music Bill said, and the people dancing…

Maurice swore to himself that he would never go out drinking with Bill again; but he'd said that the week before and it crossed his mind why he was in such un-good health. He puts on a record: it is the sad Parisian street chanteuse — Edith Piaf. The little sparrow touches his heart. It is — *La Vie en Rose*. Maurice pads over to the corner to retrieve the OPEN sign and places it out on the sidewalk serving the naked spirits of the art ghetto's abandoned landscape. He steps back in and looks at the Czech woman's paintings: "They are marvelous! Grotesque, tortured and perfect… the agony of humanity, a totalitarian abattoir of bones, sinew, meat… communism, the Nazis… Orwell… shadows going down a flight of lonely stairs, a pathetic figure cringes in a corner; it's all in red, black and gray. Nobody will ever buy any of them, but it does not matter as long as the people continue to Come and See… That is what matters… the crackling of the fissures in the frozen tundra of the reality of others. Existentialism — Nihilism — enough to get Sartre to cry for pity for mankind." (Maurice is explaining this all in French to Godot the Siamese cat who listens very attentively) "And then we've got Jessica Geiger's body of work of the dejected caste — sculptures… life-like, of the winos, the tweekers, the hookers, the bag-ladies, the neglected children with the snot dribbling down from their raw noses, and of the beaten and dazed Indians of the Street… the forgotten and the lost — what everybody does not want to see, feel — the untouchables, the fear. The respectable people from the other galleries who get lost and sometimes wind up here — flee; especially when the house band Utterance Tongue is playing — who can blame them —

Yes, this would look good in my fine living room in Bellevue." Then in English: "Yes! for you see Godot… I am a man who loves the Opera! I am an artiste!… No, I have no slides!… for it is all here!" as he points emphatically to his head as his nostrils flare and his ice blue eyes widen.

"I am a conceptual artist!"

The furrow of his brow wrinkles with fury. Godot lays on his back waiting for some rubs. The phone rings. Maurice picks it up.

"Yes, yes Parkin's Glass? Yes that was me that called… yes as soon as possible… yes as many mirrors as you have. We need them delivered. Yes walls of mirrors. They go on the ceiling. A house of glass. Thank you very much — merci beaucoup; you have been so kind. Au revoir, good-bye." Man, that daughter of Parkin's is crazy-rude, and the old lady's dressed to the nines cutting glass and the old man is out flying airplanes with Oriental hookers, what an orange asylum, right smack in the middle of Capitol Hill. Maurice says to himself as he pulls out his Zippo lighter and fires up a Pall Mall. Maurice pets Godot, the sensitive assassin, a few times rubbing him underneath the chin and then the belly. Perfunctory acknowledgement granted Maurice heads back to the area where the paint is stored, looking to see how much flat black paint is available. Not enough! Ah he walks over to the designated area serving as the kitchen. It smelled bad like a stale sickly sweet fermenting Russian perfume. He went to the Mr. Coffee. The light was on and the pot half-full.

"Messieur Mac must have made it this morning." Maurice pours himself a cup. "Aw, this goddam fucking American coffee — I will never get use to it! Thank God it is quickly becoming an endangered species on the verge of extinction here in Seattle! And now they run around self-congratulating themselves like they were the ones to invent espresso! I can't believe this shit! Aw we have to get an old espresso machine here — that way we could make a little money, aw, but this damn Manifesto Party Committee shit — I don't know why sometimes they just don't go home and make love to one another — aw alas, art and politics, politics and art, art plus money, money plus art aw it all equals the same — Corruption and Bullshit. Aw, we can't make any money cuz that's not communist, no pardon me, I mean socialist enough. Christos!"

Godot nods his head. Maurice drinks the brown water serving as coffee taking out a cigarette. The little monkey man from Belgium is solemn in his contemplation as he explores his environs for parables and paradoxes till all his focus is drawn into a clear white light. He snaps to look up at the clock realizing members of the IWW will begin arriving in another twenty minutes for their weekly meeting. And after that an NA meeting will converge — got to keep an eye on those bastards, but Maurice concedes to himself he does appreciate that 13th step — all them broken dolls. Sometimes him and Mac would catch bus #13 to the Fremont Free Baptist Church and attend the AA meetings at the old brick building — finding their higher power, seeking sanity, acknowledging the defects of their character and telling stories. Call it therapy.

"God bless the International Worker's of the World — the Wobblies!" Maurice declares aloud to Godot, "I must make a fresh pot of coffee who knows maybe we will even have customers arrive this afternoon." As Maurice is filling the coffee machine with water, Janie Jones comes a skipping on up full of enthusiasm her eyes aglow.

"Maurice! Maurice! We've begun a strike! We've begun a strike! Here are the pamphlets! I've just Xeroxed them off."

There she goes again, flashing useless parchments in his face — she doesn't even see the art and the world around her; if she wasn't so damn cute — Sweet Jane… Sweet Jane… Shangri-La… Shangri-La… Maurice takes one and thanks her, gives her a little wink and proceeds to add a little brandy to his tin coffee cup. She goes over to the big table to prepare notes and database. Members begin sauntering in — a cast of do-gooders, malcontents and lost souls looking for a cause, a sense of belonging and… free donuts, but who don't want to be cops. Maurice apprehensively reads from the manifesto: It reads in large bold print — **IWW ON STRIKE! WE ARE ON STRIKE AT SOUTH PARK MINI-MART (SPMM) BECAUSE OWNERSHIP AND MANAGEMENT HAVE REFUSED TO ACKNOWLEDGE OUR GRIEVANCES ABOUT THEIR HARASSMENT BOTH INSIDE THE WORKPLACE AND OUT ON THE PICKET LINE. THESE ACTS INCLUDE**

PHYSICAL INTIMIDATION IN THE WORKPLACE, ILLEGAL FIRINGS, SURVEILLANCE OF UNION EMPLOYEES ON AND OFF TIME, DRIVING VEHICLES OVER THE SIDEWALK TO INTIMIDATE PICKETERS, CUTTING HOURS, WITHHOLDING PAY AND NUMEROUS OTHER VIOLATIONS OF LABOR LAW.

OUR STRIKE IS NOT ABOUT WAGES, BUT IS FOR THE DIGNITY AND RESPECT AND THE RIGHTS TO ORGANIZE IN A UNION TO IMPROVE WORKING CONDITIONS. OUR MANAGER, LESTER BARCO, IS READY TO CALL THE POLICE ON US FOR THE SLIGHTEST INCIDENT (USUALLY STARTED BY CLIENTS OR FRIENDS OF MANAGEMENT) BUT WILL NOT RESPECT OUR RIGHT TO FREE SPEECH ON A PUBLIC SIDEWALK OR FOR US TO BARGAIN COLLECTIVELY.

PLEASE SUPPORT US BY NOT PURCHASING GAS OR GROCERIES AT SOUTH PARK MINI-MART, AND BY TELLING YOUR FRIENDS AND NEIGHBORS ABOUT OUR PLIGHT AND STRUGGLE. YOUR HELP IS GREATLY APPRECIATED AND MEANS A LOT. YOUR SUPPORT WILL ALSO MEAN A SPEEDY END TO THIS CONFLICT, SO THAT WE CAN GO BACK TO WORK AND TAKE CARE OF OUR NEEDS.

THANK YOU

SOUTH PARK MINI-MART UNION EMPLOYEES

(On the back of the page it reads)

IF YOU WOULD LIKE TO SHOW YOUR SUPPORT FOR OUR RIGHTS TO ORGANIZE IN THE WORKPLACE, YOU CAN LET THE MANAGEMENT AND OWNERSHIP OF THE SOUTH PARK MINI-MART KNOW HOW YOU FEEL.

JOHNNY FRIDAY (OWNER OF ALL-TOGETHER TRAVEL AND SOUTH PARK MINI-MART)

4389 CALIFORNIA AVE W SEATTLE, WA 98136

PHONE # @ ALL-TOGETHER: (206) 448-4370

PHONE # @ HOME (206) 837-9030

LESTER BARKO, MANAGER

19201 22ND AVE E

SEATTLE, WA 98102

PHONE # @ SOUTH PARK MINI-MART (206) 867-5309

IF YOU WOULD LIKE MORE INFORMATION ON OUR UNION; THE INDUSTRIAL WORKERS OF THE WORLD, OR LEARN ABOUT HOW TO ORGANIZE AT YOUR OWN JOB, PLEASE CALL JOE HILL @ 723-4747!

"Ah this is all well and good Janie but the power of the workers is not rooted in organization, but in disruption." Maurice then remembers his dinner appointment at the Tai Tung with Baby Nambu and grabs the telephone to confirm reservations. Brother Maurice with a hop and a skip saunters on down the street like a spring lamb, heading towards Chinatown singing a happy little tune in French: *Contre les Viets* —

"Against the Viets, against the enemy. Wherever duty calls us, Soldiers of France, soldiers of our country. We mount toward the firing line" — He abruptly stops in front of the Bread of Life Mission, listening in on the preacher's energetic message: "You see here sinners!" he shouts down, red-faced and wild-eyed at the shuffling drab of gray anonymous men... waiting... waiting... waiting for their hot meal.

"He left Heaven's glory and came down to this earth, went to Calvary's Cross to pay your debt of sin. He hung on that cross between heaven and earth and between two thieves in your place and stead. God laid upon him all your inequity Isaiah 53:6."

"Now you may have eternal by taking your place as a lost sinner and by faith accepting this gift of all gifts, Jesus Christ, as your our savior John 3:16. Will you take Him as your Savior? Friends don't turn him away. He is waiting to receive you. He is longing to bless and save you. He wants to give Eternal Life to you, and if you accept Him, he will fill your soul with a joy such as you have never known in your life, and make you a child of God, and heir of God and a joint heir with Jesus Christ — Romans 8:17. Amen and allelooyah! Brothers and Sisters!"

With that the lost sinner Brother Maurice turns his back in disgust and walks on saying, "Ai! Och! the turning of one's sickness into virtue — that ought to wet some appetites for the brothers and sisters. But the Blacks, they are the backbone of this country — Really... and everybody knows..."

Like an apache of the Paris underworld, Maurice recalls scenes from the French Connection but they're not from the movie — they're from his life; thinking of that zombie/punk rocker staggering down the Marseilles street as a lean man from Curacao comes running down the cobble-stoned street and smacks him down a few more times and then flicks the knife out to stab him and finish the job that quiet morning. Maurice for some reason, grabs him by the arm, "Arret." Just as a Renault full of his brethen comes speeding up and he jumps in and they take off. And the zombie staggers on unconsciously to his eternity. That quiet morning. He doesn't know why that episode came to him, he walks by the methadone clinic and past the stocky guy in camies and a Mohawk who is shouting invectives about his lack of meds — the lights are on but nobody is home. Across the street a natty-haired barefooted woman crack addict is rolling a half-passed out drunk who swats at her occasionally as she purloins thru his pockets. She then squats and takes a pee right on the sidewalk. "Ai humanity!" Maurice shakes his head, the half-passed out drunk reminds him of a few Legionnaires he use to know and the crack addict reminds him of a woman back in Djibouti he use to frequent... and sometimes she would take his money just about like that. Maurice begins another happy little tune — "Nous sommes de la Legion" — We are the Legion. So far from our homes. To the front we will march. To defeat our enemy. With our arms, with our hearts and with our lives... We will defend France against her enemies...

After stopping in front of the Publix Bar contemplating a relaxing libation, Maurice, takes out a cig and fires it up with his Zippo lighter and looks at his watch and decides not to keep Baby Nambu waiting at the old Gambling Club. He begins to turn around to face the last glowing shards of light from the iron sun as it dips behind the dungy monolithic concrete hulk called the Kingdome, past the

Dome Stadium Tavern, past Ruby Chau's Cafe, past the poor old Wah-Mee, past the Tai Tung Restaurant. He whistles as he saunters by the closing fruit and vegetable hawkers of Chinatown, some yell to Maurice, "Hey Ong Chun!" (big boss in Vietnamese) as he enters the club to be greeted by a big generous smile from Baby Nambu. It is the Year of the Hare in the Chinese calendar.

"Hey Belgy!"

"Ca gaze," with a flat-handed salute.

Maurice grimaces at this hey Belgy business of Baby Nambu's but has never seemed to break him of this insipid American habit of nicknames and fucked-up sobriquets. Bringing his forefinger up: "Yes, I am a Belgian, I am a Walloon to be more precise and my name is Maurice and I am a citizen of France. But the Legion is my country." With that last statement Maurice's chest swelled as his heart was proud... all this just made Baby Nambu grin even wider. They clinked the drinks that Baby Nambu had already waiting at the bar.

"Salud."

"Salud."

"And how was your latest trip to the Maghreb my good friend?"

"The flight into Benghazi with the 707 went smooth. The German and Icelander brokered a neat deal with a letter of credit and a slick end-user certificate destined for Chad and some good Soviet stuff — AK-47s, machine guns, grenade launchers, and shoulder-fired anti-aircraft rockets. Sam's got the inside with CENZIN — AKMS-47 assault rifles in quantity for only $150 a pop! And good Chi-Com stuff too."

"Love that Foreign Material Acquisition program, working it in with those ag credits." Maurice recalls first encountering Baby Nambu back at Takhli in Thailand when he was a pilot for Air America, doin regular rice drops to guarantee an adequate food supply so the Hmong of Laos would be free to devote all their energies to fighting the Pathet Lao and opium production — all part of the politics of heroin. Wait till we get to Afghanistan and deal with the Taliban — then the smack will really begin to flow again here in Junkiedom U.S.A... like back in the day when Phoumi Novasan, the big fat man who liked to dine and to wench was running things for Colby in the Golden Triangle. Ah, sometimes if he could just play bocce on the sand back in l'Aquitaine with his Corsican friends, but ah alas, no Maurice was in the milieu... And then, later on in Rhodesia, Baby Nambu and Maurice found themselves gainfully employed as soldiers of fortune where Mac had already set up shop with those British mercs and Gurkhas. But that was a long time ago and it's not true... Nambu was a good pilot, a damn good pilot. But a horrible driver.

"Algeria?" Maurice inquires.

"Bad."

"And Didier?"

"No word."

"No word?... where is the man? How about Le Mere?"

"You haven't heard? He be dead — like Elvis. Mac delivered his will to his parents in Quebec a month before he crashed his Ducati at 147 miles per hour."

"Oh no! — this breaks my heart, he saved me in Panama — pound for pound the toughest Marine. He was un bon baroudeur. How did Mac not mention it?! Zut alors! Ai! we will throw a three day Irish wake for our Quebecois Metis. With much whiskey! So what happened in Algeria?"

"Mujahedeen were waiting on the beach for Echo Force."

"Wha-aht?! You must be joking... body count? how many casualties?"

"Amazingly only two wounded, but they didn't stick around too long, but God knows how many mujahedeen — beaucoup fellaghas fell. What I saw from the sub looked like a major Fourth of July celebration. 'Course you know, they were — waiting for air cover... *xin loi.** "

"Ai — *bien sur*, but of course, *xin loi* mutherfuckers... they were — waiting for air cover. I know about that all too well like you

* *'too bad' in Vietnamese*

my bon pal, promises, promises… Och! this world we live in … it's upside down. So I take it you didn't sell a great deal of computers," chortles Maurice as he looks intently into the opaque eyes of Baby Nambu. His skin dark like a Navajo, you couldn't tell by looking at him that he was pushing fifty years of age — not thirty, only vaguely around the eyes could one discern the traces. 'Course as Maurice liked to point out — he didn't dye his hair black like Baby Nambu, but still nobody would ever mistake Maurice for a guy pushing thirty, black hair or not.

"Pas beaucoup pour les computers."

"Another round of Johnny Walkers si vous plais," then Maurice turns back to Baby Nambu and says, "in two months there is going to be the big WTO meeting here at the Convention Center in Seattle. Our good old friend Hank will be arriving as a celebrated guest speaker. Sonbitch — Paris Peace Talks — Merde! Beat the devil — he sold us out! And Laos and Cambodia. Just like DeGaulle did to us in Algeria; the poor pied noirs. We had won! 'Cept for the unprecedented malevolence of the world press. Africa — a cold country with a hot sun. I cannot forget leaving the revetments at Elaine and Isabelle, going through the wire — making our way to the jungle to escape Giap and the Viet Minh. La agonie… Diem Bien Phu. I was sixteen years old — a runaway." Maurice hisses under his breath. "Ai, this country is too much — the American Way… is to seduce a man by bribery and make a prostitute out of him. The cafard… one has to question the futility of one's existence… a contagious madness. The government keeps declaring a war on drugs and a war on the mob they insist exists when they should be waging war on poverty and ignorance. These are adverse conditions. But if you did something that society say you shouldn't have done, you have to be prepared to accept it, innocent or guilty. That's what being a man is all about. You know, everybody talks the talk, but when it comes down to walkin the walk, they fall on their faces. Everybody ain't what they say. That's the problem."

Nambu takes a deep drag off his Dunhill cigarette while gazing across at the bar's mirror. Goddam orientalism, can't read a clue as to what Nambu is thinking Maurice says to himself. Nothing was said for a long time. They just slowly sipped their whiskeys, smoking contemplatively.

"Let's meet at the Place Pigalle next — I always feel so warm, comfortable and at home there and the pinard is exquisite."

"Yeah, I get a warm fuzzy feeling there too, especially with the busted windows, cocaine on the mirrors and nice farang crowd."

"Inch'Allah."

"Inch'Allah."

"Merde."

the food bank:

Makin the rounds with Mac being Mac's official designated driver, Walter would often find himself up at the University District food bank — one of Mac's jobs — so Thursday morning when the trucks arrived for delivery; Walter had inadvertently become a "volunteer" at the food bank in the last few weeks and let us preface a "volunteer" being someone who did not understand the question. One old raspy codger had asked him what he was in for because a lot of the volunteers were working off jail time thru community service. (Trimsetter Corporation was not happy with his frequent Thursday tardiness or outright absences, but he was a temp and good help was hard to find so even bad help had a job) Walter is initially shocked by the blunt supposition that he is some sort of lumpen proletariat criminal, but regains his composure and casually replies,

"Drugs — Rape... Mur-der... it's just a kiss away..." which makes the grizzled old codger's eyes pop as big as planets as he hurriedly distances himself thru busy-ness from Walter arranging these cans of beans over here and those cans of corn over there. After that the poor old pain in the ass codger whose name was Mort never ever turned his back on Walter — don't smoke dope, don't drop the soap. But Walter mostly worked with a large Samoan, but kind of small for a Samoan, guy named Andy who had a big old pumpkin head and a smile like a big old scary jack-o-lantern. In fact, the circumference of Andy's head was bigger than Walter's whole ass (Walter did suffer from flat-ass syndrome). This guy is big, the man has girth, but he maybe 5' 10" in height. Walter and him did most of the hand stow under Mac's directorship and outstanding Marxist leadership which made Walter realize: so it is better to be bossed by men of little faith, who set their hearts on toys, than men animated by lofty ideals who are ready to ruthlessly sacrifice themselves and others for dedication to a holy cause. The most formidable employer is he who like Stalin or Pol-Pot who casts himself in the role of a representative and champion of the workers — Trimsetter was so ineffectual compared to the lash of Mac.

They usually had one or two guys helping them out doing their community service trip, but sometimes it was just them. Andy always seemed to be hustling Walter about something.

"You! You go and get the car, bring it back to the alley here! Then I can load up all this food that come in — good steaks! I give you some."

Walter got a perplexed look on his face — he realizes Andy has a very large family; one or two different relatives were always showing up every Thursday, but this was a food bank — they give food away here. It really didn't seem necessary to steal the food from the food bank at least Walter didn't think so.

Andy, uh, this is a food bank. How come whenever I bring Mac's car around I feel like I'm involved in crime — like a hijack?"

The alley and the environs behind the food bank did actually have the natural grace of a crime scene.

"Like Andy — do you get it — we're working at a food bank that gives food away for free to people and we're stealing food that is free…"

"No, no, no you just go and get the Green Hornet and park it over here. Some nice salmon just showed up — big fish."

Big fish for big people. Sometimes earnest Walter was just pretty fuckin white, but reluctantly Walter always yielded to the pressure and relented and would go get the Ambassador — curious what Mac was thinking of this whole operation. I mean a couple of grocery sacks, but the whole trunk and car filled to the brim... whole 100 pound sacks of potatoes and onions, five or six frozen whole salmon, crates of milk, cases of canned goods, blocks of government cheese. Recently, some of the paid regular staff had been getting a little suspicious. It was getting pretty flagrant. Mac seemed mostly concerned that there wasn't enough room left in the car seat for him to sit down in.

And then, of course, like a confederacy of dunces, there is the strange litany of street theatre that abounds in the University District — Mac seemed to have his own special clients — an MK/ULTRA victim with his long gray/brown hair down to the middle of his back and his saucer-sized 70s plastic spectacles came clamoring up the alley toward Andy and Walter picking thru the dumpsters.

"Where's that one guy?"

"Who?" Walter replies looking at Andy who just shrugs.

"The guy who wears the jungle-green bandanna — he's a hunter!"

Walter looks at Andy who goes from bewilderment to letting fly his biggest, joyous grin. "Mac?"

"Yeah the hunter — the man is a hunter."

Mac is frantically mouthing, NO NO NO from inside the door. Andy is just smiling wider.

"No, Mac is not here."

"Where is he?"

"He's meeting with Henry Kissinger."

"Oh," and with that perfectly reasonable explanation the client commences to walk away, picking up a few cans as he goes in a zig-zag pattern down the alley inhaling more symptomatic nerve gas.

"Nice work Walt buddy, good thinkin on your feet," as Mac slips in from the shadows.

"Yeah Gustav will be back in an hour or so asking for my whereabouts — telling him I'm having a cocktail meeting with Dr. Henry Kissinger is a great one — probably like de-programs him a little bit. That's just brilliant. Hey dog, I've got a deal with the Russian horde today after the street urchins get thru. Man, those Russians got no manners — like a football game. Worse thing Reagan ever did was bring down that wall. You're going to finish unloading this last truck — I'll meet you later down at the Last Exit for a cup of coffee and a game of mah-jong and some pai-gow with the rest of the miscreants of the U-District. There's someone I want you to meet — Cat O Nine, he'll see you before you see him so there is no use in giving you a description of him. Too-rah loo-rah, loo-rah." O the premonitions — what could that possibly mean Walter wonders as he stumbles down Brooklyn Ave in the U-District and comes upon Cat who gives him a nod as he most flagrantly deals in substantial weed in the old brick courtyard with some young aspiring hippies. Walter rolls himself a cigarette and waits.

Chapter Two

Po' Bukra

The Ozarks:

From the dark woods of a nearby hillside, Louis Willy is giggling himself silly till near he's wetting his pants with the incessant sniggering which is only occasionally broken up by great heaves of exasperated laughing followed by a blood-curdling howl or two. He has just burned down the trailer park. It had been a dream and now it was a reality and joy, a precious, precious joy fulfilled. In the black and green of his camo make-up and gear, Louis Willy reminded one of a chattering scraggly raccoon.

He had grown up there as a child. Physically from a distance, the surroundings about the trailer park was an idyllic quaint wooded holler, but upon closer exam of the locale one took notice of details of abject grounded-out to the dirt poverty; bent TV antennas and broken down cars, empty bottles of beer and soda pop cans strewn amongst the weed patches and dog shit-filled lots full of mean little boys and mangy stray dogs. Buncha po' bukra* amidst aluminum tin-wrapped wikiups shrouded in a constant smoky haze of pungent burning plastic garbage from rusted fifty gallon steel barrels… with shards of broken glass and community bulletins. But alas Paradise not no more. Willy shook with glee. The little poor unhappy soul.

The townies of Mena had always referred to it as Goosepecker till it had come true and that's what was written for address upon the letters from cousins from Detroit and St. Louis. All those memories going up in flames — a few good, but mostly bad. It was cathartic for Louis Willy as he looks on at the bright yellow and orange flames and hears the shouts and cries of the few tenants around. Most were down at the county fair. But soon there was a whole mess of them showing up. Louis Willy knew that most of them did not deserve this; it was just bad luck and guilt by association. But Louis Willy had had a lot of bad luck and that place had been a major component to it, so many daddies later couldn't none keep track a how many, "Boy u git sweeping now!" "But who are you?" "I met your mom at the bus stop; I'm your daddy now — do what I say" — thus it served as a good start for his campaign of righteous retribution — burnin down the trailer park!! But it was all going to be for the good of America! — this cleansing; he'd seen the planes flying in at night from Central America, he'd seen the Contras and Black Water training — nearly got caught one night spying. Did get picked up one afternoon, told them he was just out squirrel hunting, "Nuthin wrong with that — been huntin these hills my whole life…" he had his little Winchester .22 pump along with three dead squirrels and a possum in the gunny sack, but the Blackwater goons still absconded off with his binoculars. He was going to get back at those Blackwater boys. Louis Willy, as he thinks to his self, he knew that the hills did have eyes in more than one way, as said earlier; he'd been hunting in these hills for his whole life, and now revenue agents from the

* po' bukra is what the African slaves called thems peoples in the woods who liked to do nothing more than raise a few hogs, hunt, race horses, gamble, shoot their guns, drink whiskey and fight all the time — the plantation owners considered enslaving these slackers — the Civil War put a halt to those plans.

government showing up all over the place, black helicopters buzzing around scaring the game, people disappearing, lots of curious hunting accidents had been occurring the last couple of years — never use to have so many accidents — I been sending my reports to the Posse Comitatus, let'em know what I know — God! Folk! Nation! — they're taking our land! Maybe we need to mobilize the Arkansas National Guard — send them to Honduras or Iraq — off to war. He couldn't wait to get back and tell his cousin Roy what he had done and what was to be done — for the Cause. Roy had bad memories of the trailer park and hated it as well. Louis Willy scrambled up the hill thru the bush back towards the direction of the compound. He knew he'd have to get moving. Maybe go visit Cousin Alfred in Detroit first, before making it to Seattle. He was making tracks.

Well, Louis Willy made the haste to his cousin Roy DePugh's and that just turned out to be a big mistake. Barely had time to buy some dog food before catchin the Greyhound to Detroit. It was all in the local papers the next day along with the story about the trailer park at Goosepecker burning down "Arson Suspected!" But this other story happen to work out as a kind of a neat diversion for Louis Willy because it took the headlines and kept the deputies a little more occupied: Man Killed After Chainsaw Incident. Smithville — Argument between two roommates left one dead from a shotgun blast to the chest after simmering dispute was settled last Saturday morning in doublewide located on the edge of town. Dwight Patterson, 27, was killed after he tried to use a chainsaw to get past the bedroom door of his roommate Roy Depugh.

"Two roommates got into a dispute, apparently one that had been brewing for some time and then it came to a head," said Sheriff Leon Carter.

Six people apparently live in the enclave. While the initial cause of the incident is unclear, what is known is that Patterson wanted to enter the bedroom of his housemate — the door was locked however.

According to Deputy C.W. Buckner, Patterson picked up his chainsaw and told another housemate, "Get out of the house, things are going to get rough." A fourth roommate was loading things into his pickup truck outside and Patterson's girlfriend was sleeping in another room when Patterson started the chainsaw and began cutting into DePugh's bedroom door.

"Don't!" Depugh reportedly yelled at his housemate several times as Patterson continued cutting thru the door. Depugh, 33 years of age, was waiting for Patterson inside his room with a double-barreled shotgun.

Patterson was shot once in the chest upon entrance to the room. Later, police pronounced him dead at the scene. Depugh fled taking the shotgun with him. The roommate loading the pickup truck went to search for the sheriff in nearby Mena; there was no telephone in the double-wide nor in any of the outbuildings of the compound. The roommate found Deputy Lester Bangs and led him back to the scene. Police said that as the two were driving back to the residence, they spotted Depugh strolling along Rural Route 14. He was unarmed. The sheriff says Depugh is charged with homicide while Depugh claims he was standing his ground and shot in self-defense.

Officers are unaware of how long the two had been quarreling. The story Patterson's girlfriend Wendy Williams told the deputies differed greatly from the other witnesses, but the peace officers said she was hysterical and not making sense when they first questioned her. Police say some drinking had been going on and that it's possible some of the residents were drug users with evidence of the manufacture of meth although drug use has not been determined as a factor in the shooting. Witnesses told the police that Mr. Patterson had been behaving particularly peculiar for the last month. They said he had been seeing imaginary people running in the woods and would shoot at them with his guns as well as claiming to fire upon mysterious black helicopters and unidentified airplanes. The Sheriff was also told that he threatened to shoot his girlfriend. The trailer/compound area is called Tobacco Road and sits on a relatively secluded tree-filled lot. The nearest neighbors live at least a half mile away.

The premises are surrounded by broken down cars, two ancient travel trailers, no small amount of junk, a couple of tar-paper shacks, a tarped-off party spot over the remains of a burnt cabin and a rather sophisticated earthen bunker full of guns and ordnance of which the proper authorities such as the ATF and DEA are further investigating into as well as gathering evidence from the various bathtubs and lab equipment for the manufacture of meth. It seems that some of the witnesses disappeared later that evening; one being a Louis Willy, 29 years of age, a cousin of Roy Depugh's who may have possibly shot at roommate and witness who drove off in the pickup truck to get the police. Mr. Willy is also wanted for questioning in regards to the fire that encapsulated the trailer park at Goosepecker. Authorities believe it was arson.

"Yeah, that sumbitch was lucky," Louis Willy says to himself, "if I'd a been able to get another round off I'd a plugged him straight to hell, but I couldn't find the damn right bullets for this 30-06 Government. Goddam bullets everywhere; should have grabbed that rocket-launcher."

Louis Willy had woken up in the bunker, from his moonshine whiskey stupor to the sound of a chainsaw — most proximate to his very whereabouts. He immediately grabbed a Mini-14 jumping around back and forth several times waving the gun erratically presuming it was a raid and that agents of the FBI would come bursting in at any moment. But nobody did. Then the shotgun blast and Louis Willy became cognizant of who was doing the yelling and screaming as the hounds howled and the banshees wailed. Hearing the pickup truck begrudgingly cranking over Louis Willy runs over to look out one of the gun ports. Beginning to ascertain the situation, realizing Toby is off to get the Po-lice! and this would mean bad trouble for Cousin Roy — Louis Willy runs outside and points from the hip with a Mini-14 to shoot out the tires, but the damn thing jams so he runs back inside and grabs the Remington bolt-action 30-06 looking for cartridges finally finding a box, scrambling back to the gun port, peering out down the dirt road as the old International, by now about seventy yards away; Louis Willy breathes, takes proper aim and fires. Misses the whole damn thing — didn't even nick it — if only he hadn't been generally discharged from the Army and had been able to go to sniper school like he'd always wanted to do. 'Course dawn was just greeting the morning and he'd had a little to drink, but Louis Willy convinced himself he had at least hit the truck even though he was aiming for Toby's head. Tryin to do it just like G. Gordon Liddy would do it — aim straight for the federales head. As the coon hounds continue braying and howling, Wendy's hysterical screaming pierces Willy's ears; seems she's just realizing her boyfriend Patterson has just taken a 12 gauge blast on full choke of double-odd buckshot to the chest. Louis Willy again ambles out of the bunker now armed with a 9mm Luger still wondering what's going on, firing at anything that moves, killing one chicken, droppin one possum in a tree, and wounding two pigs till he sees Roy come placidly out onto the porch carrying a smoking shotgun.

"Louis! What the hell are you doin?!"

"Well, well, I wake up and I hear all this racket and a chainsaw, bloodhounds, gunshots and hollering and figures we's gettin invaded… and Toby takes off in the old International… so I shot at him."

"Nah that methed-out, dumb-ass Patterson decided to attack me with a chainsaw… thought I was gettin fresh with Wendy…"

"She likes a good beatin' every once in a while…" Louis interjects.

"Put that pistol down… you probably best git your ass scarce from this scene… and now I got an upset woman. I think I'll go walk on down the road and have me a smoke and a Mountain Dew… I just don't know sometimes… I just don't know; seems like the whole world is just goin crazy. Ought to just go back to distillin shine and growin weed — this meth shit. Just don't know… guess, we'll play that dead man's song, turn those speakers up full blast… play it all night long… play that dead man's song, just don't know…" Southern culture — on the skids… Probably time to go watch some dirt-track racin. Cook up some succotash.

Pulling out of the bus depot in Little Rock, with his haversack, large bag of dry dog food and big Mason jar of vitamin C, Louis Willy stares out the window. Well, he was just plum damn glad to get the hell out of there — makin his escape from rural dementia, thems peoples are crazee! Got me here this special ticket from Greyhound, can get me to wherever I want to go here in this United States of America for $99 for 30 days. Should be in Detroit by tomorrow morning — I hope Cousin Alfred hasn't moved.

Chapter Three

Kwameland

"One day you and I will occupy the White House and peasants will drool with envy. Until then do your best to remain a virgin."

in a letter from John Hinkley to Jodie Foster

Detroit Greyhound bus depot:

Louis Willy took out some spare change like the only change he had ever had and took the phone number from a piece of paper he had in his billfold, people were staring at him, at least, Louis believed they were. The phone begins ringing.

"Hello Alfred, that you? Yeah, this is Louis your old cousin from Goosepecker — I'm in Detroit right now down here at the bus depot. Can you pick me up? None of your cars are running... but I could walk there but I'd better take the bus... ok ok what bus number? Yeah, yeah I got some money — been choppin wood. No everybody's fine. Roy shot a man the other day, but it was in self-defense — you remember Patterson? Yeah Elvira's son — been acting real crazy lately, but a lot of weird stuff been goin on in the hills lately. Contras everywhere, helicopters and planes at night, Blackwater ninja guys runnin around scarin the game and more suits in mirrored sunglasses in great big black SUVs than Louisiana coon asses... yeah, yeah the hills have eyes. Damn Revenue agents! Where's Bill Clinton when you need him? Hell he's probably right here on a date in Dee-troit... dancin with some colored girl... Ok I take a right on Lafayette Blvd just pass John K. King's Books. So Alfred, yeah I'll see ya soon."

Louis Willy is waiting for his bus. He walks by a homeless-looking Mexican laborer playin' some mean licks out there a buskin like ol' Bob Dylan, sweet as sugar, like bluegrass. Louis got his "stuff" (what he was meanin) and gave him a couple of bucs. A little fracas erupts in the parking lot of the Greyhound bus depot. The blue uniformed security guards come out and are trying to escort some fierce looking, red bandanna on his head, red-faced large ruffian off the premises. Louis wonders if he should intercede. He figures he is better armed than the security and he has his handcuffs and his license to carry as well as his private detective certificate of authorization card (mail order), but the bus pulls up and he elects to get on while the gettin is good. He's the only Caucasian-type looking person on the bus, but he don't mind. He's just lookin out the window; never been to Dee-troit before. Might have to do some kinda autopsy on the city by the looks of things. He's trying to mind his own business stroking his scraggly brown squirrel scruff of a beard when some yackety-yack from some older gentleman looking like he's in his mid-fifties commences to jeer at Louis Willy with the un-subtle pronouncement to the rest of the bus riders that Louis Willy is CIA.

"Yeah this dude here's CIA — CIA doin the Man's work here spyin on us... here in the occupied zone... He's come down to the ghetto all dressed up in disguise, but I can tell you — you CIA, Chuck! You don't fool me in that hillbilly outfit of yours... u justgarbledeegoogah-gahmofodooGAHhhh... ha-ha!"

The guy is hard to understand he is so loaded on wine and whatever else. Louis Willy just looks straight ahead beginning to boil with righteous anger — justified.

"Shee-eet CIA right here on da bus MK Ultra mutherfukkuh... FBI, Co-Intelpro, Henry Kissinger Tri-Lateral, New World Order agent provocateur… name's probably David Rockefeller or some-thin!"

Of course, some of the folks on the bus are beginning to laugh with the show.

"Lionel why don't you just sit down and shut up." The bus driver tells him. That just brings on more laughter as it just feeds into brother Lionel's show. Louis Willy begins to envision a hostage crisis situation; maybe if they get near a McDonald's he'll do it… he just shot at one man the other day. Happy meals for everyone.

Then Louis Willy explodes into a gibbering jumbled mishmash of words and symbols and hillbilly expletives, "Sumbitch! No CIA! Why don't you mind your own business!… am private detective… licensed to carry!… make citizen's arrest!" as he bares his teeth and begins frothing at the mouth enough that Mister Lionel and others begin to move away from Louis Willy in fear of catching rabies and leave him quite alone. The bus becomes as mute as an eggplant. It abruptly comes to the stop where Louis Willy is designated to disem-bark. He does so peacefully and everybody in the bus is very relieved that the little nuclear white boy does so.

"Thank you mam," he says to the large bus driver.

Carrying his haversack, Louis Willy eyes about the semi-vacant streets suspiciously. Tumbleweed bounces about the empty ware-houses as the skyscrapers loom like giant vertical gray glass tombs. He is suppose to be looking for a large building called Joe Louis Arena and to go left from there till he hits the Kronk's Boxing Gym and then head south a few blocks. Louis Willy is talking to himself as he walks giving himself the directions. Can't miss it from there Cousin Alfred sez, eventually I'm to see a sign with the name Pease on it. Louis Willy, with Confederate beard upon his face, ambles pigeon-toed down the street still feeling a little outnumbered. Look-ing around him it was apparent to Louis Willy that America loves black people as much as it loves hillbillies — my gawd there ain't no white people here in Detroit he was beginning to think. Appears a little afro-centric. Kwanzaa is very celebrated here he thought. Louis Willy had always thought Santa Claus and God were one and the same — probably about fifteen years old when he figured it out that it wasn't so. They're two different people.

He just keeps on going down the road hoping nobody will hassle him. He gets to the Kronk's and heads south and goes on a few more blocks. The late afternoon sun is burning through making it strangely muggy. He walks upon his hobnailed boots looking for a sign that says Pease on it and then he comes upon a piece of bare old plywood with the faded name written on it in orange spray paint. Alfred is in front looking under the hood of a Pontiac with some skinny guy.

"Cousin Alfred!"

"Is that you Louis? Look at that beard! hee hee hoo hoo! You been cuttin that with a dull pine cone? Looks like you just seen a hoop snake after rasslin with a pack of rabid possums! hee hee hoo hoo!" The other fellow stood there bucktoothed and grinning, guzzling on a can of Falstaff smoking a cigarette. Louis didn't think his beard looked that bad. Big Cousin Alfred took a spit off his tobacco and come up to shake Louis's hand wiping off some of the oil and grease off his hands onto his gray Detroit Lion's t-shirt.

"No you look good Louis you look good by gum… all growed up. Hoo hoo hee hee I just didn't wake up this morning expecting to get a call from kin telling me they were visitin Dee-troit. Hoo hoo hee hee u wanna beer or a grape Nehi?"

It was a happy reunion after that first grape soda. Sharin' old stories with some of the kin; two in particular stood out in Louis Willy's mind as particularly funny. Alfred told them well — one was about the preacher and the lady, and it was a true story, up near Coon Creek lived a widow-woman named Twohig and the other women didn't like her, but the menfolk all thought she was wonderful. There was men right here in town that would sneak out and leave their wife pretty near every night, and old Braxton Bragg used to lock up his store and go see the widow in broad daylight. Them fellows burnt up the Coon Creek road all the time, and they didn't care who knowed it, neither. The womenfolk all says the Widow Twohig ought to be throwed in jail, but the sheriff wouldn't do nothing, because he was pussy-simple too. So then a bunch of church people went to see the preacher, which his name was Wilkes. They wanted him to tell the Widow-woman she better behave herself, or else move away. Because if she don't, the decent women is going to give the widow Twohig a horse-whipping, and then run her out of the country. Old Preacher Wilkes grumbled a good deal, but finally he say he'll go on up Coon Creek and see about it. Young Park Armstrong takes the preacher out here with his horse and buggy. When they got to the Widow Twohig's cabin Park just waited outside, and Old Man Wilkes was a long time. Finally, he comes back out back out, a shaking his head. "Mistress Twohig is a good Christian woman," he says, "cultured and refined, the best you ever seen! I don't understand why the ladies are telling them bad stories about her?!"

So the preacher just stood there, a-looking at the widow woman's house on Coon Creek. "All right, Reverend," says young Park Armstrong. "Just button up your pants and we'll get home in time for supper."

Hoo hoo hee hee they all went just a knee-slapping with their grape Nehis and moonshine.

"Oh and how about this story…" went on Alfred, "you remember… let's trade twitches… that one time a fellow from Springfield come down to the James River, and some peckerwoods was having a square dance. Most of them was drinking out of fruit-jars, and it looked like they was kind of a wild bunch. Soon as a set was over the fiddlers would play a few bars of "Old Horny," and then every man grabbed a girl and took her out in the brush.

Pretty soon the city fellow begun to feel his corka-bobbing, so the next time "Old Horny" come around he picked out a likely-looking girl. When they got to the brush he says, "Are you married?" and the girl answered, "Nope." Then he says, "Do you want to do a little fucking?" and the girl answered, "Yep." So she hoisted up her dress and flopped on the ground. He pulled down his pants and started to mount her. Just as the girl was a-guiding his tallywhacker home, somebody tapped the city fellow on the shoulder.

"Excuse me mister," says one of them big peckerwoods, "would you mind trading twitches? It's pretty dark back there. I've made a mistake and picked my own sister!"

Hoo hoo — Hee hee! Oh how they all laughed — drinkin that Mountain Dew, grape soda and moonshine… "Don't worry Louis, Kwame will take care of everything… Hoo hoo hee hee. Let's go the bar and have a few stiff ones in remembrance of our kin who battled and fought hard in the War of Northern Aggression — we didn't ever even own no slaves. Off to the Old Miami. Play some snooker."

It was good to see — bounty hunting was going good for Cousin Alfred. Even had his self a big pretty Cadillac, an Eldorado '73 — didn't run, but shore looked nice…

Out there: in the Empty Quarter

Louis Willy felt a strong need for a cigarette as he sat armed with three pistols on the rapidly moving Greyhound bus. He had a .38 snub-nose Smith & Wesson revolver under his left arm pit and a Glock 20 under the right with a two-shot .32 caliber derringer wrapped around his left calf under his camies. He also carried a can of mace and two knives, a Buck and a Bowie, as well as pills against mosquito death. Louis Willy was ready for whatever, for eternal vigilance is the price of liberty as far as he saw it. And, he is licensed to carry a concealed weapon because you just never know… ground zero, the reds, the Chi-coms, the li-ber-als, homoschectuals, Zionists in conspire, hippies, the Trilateralist government; could be a hostage crisis situation at your friendly neighborhood McDonald's, could happen on this Greyhound bus. So far so good. Louis Willy is glad to be on the road and glad to have left Detroit — them peoples are crazee! Yeah, he was westering, westering across the blistering prairies, raging rivers, towering mountains — headed for Beulah land — facing starvation, Indians, rustlers, and plague. But the greatest danger was not in the wilderness. It was in Louis Willy's own untamed heart.

Somewhere in the Dakotas: Louis Willy wakes up abruptly to some young kid shouting, "Mama! Mama! Look at the bears! Look at the bears!"

"They're not bears! Those are cows!" Louis turns taciturnly to the young boy and his mama who got on in Chicago. As he turns back around he mutters under his breath,

"Stupid kid…" The mama just glares at his scraggly head and scrawny neck, but refrains from physical violence.

"Now, now honey… those are not bears, those are cows just like the little crazy cracker says." She coos to her child and says it loud enough for Louis Willy to hear. Louis hrrumphs a bit and decides to ignore like he really had a choice. He nods out, falls asleep and has dreams of lions and tigers and bears.

Louis wakes up from his slumber to see that a woman with a little too much make-up and a little too much stress on her face has gotten on the bus and is sitting across from him. He thinks her looks have the lust of a wanton. He grabs a milk-bone and pops a vitamin C and washes it down with a little purple Kool-Aid. Should hit Seattle by tomorrow morning. Louis Willy stares out the smudgy window looking up at the rising moon deep down realizing he knew about as much about that there pretty disc in the air as that cow in the field. Really man, he hopes he didn't catch any diseases in that last depot restroom in Montana — bugs everywhere! Hate havin to go in those places, makin a drop and all. He'd thought he'd try and hold out until Seattle… but it'd been three days already. The bind was awful. Louis Willy flips on the light and begins reading this book he picked up in cold, cold Billings. It is titled — U.S. on the Moon: What it Means to Us.

"In the early days of the space age, there were real fears that the Soviet Union's lead would enable the Russians to establish control of the moon. When any potential adversary can operate in an environment where we cannot, it is a matter of great concern to military planners. Now, an international treaty signed by both the United States and the Soviet Union, forbids placing weapons in space or on the moon. It also prohibits a country from making territorial claims on the moon. From a technical viewpoint, it would be possible to establish missile launching pads on the moon to send bombs against targets on earth. The best insurance we have against this happening is the moon's great distance from us. If an intercontinental missile were fired at the United States from the Soviet Union, we might have no more than 15 minutes warning, because the approaching warhead is shielded from radar detection by the horizon until it is in the later phase of its flight.

On the other hand, a missile launched from the moon to the earth could probably be detected two or three days before arrival giving time for defensive missiles to be launched to intercept it in space. By the same token, it offers no advantage to use the moon for spying on earth when this can be done infinitely better by satellites in low earth orbit."

Louis Willy closed the book. He'd had enough. Reagan was right; you get that StarWars technology. They didn't never go to the moon no how anyway. It was all a hoax staged by Hollywood in conspire with the government. All fake, saw it on a TV documentary; it never happened. Louis did believe that the Soviets had sent that Laika up into space. Couldn't get that Laika back though — poor little thing: brave dog, dead dog. He thought maybe they sent that monkey up into space as well, but he wasn't sure. He always felt sorry for that baby monkey left alone without a mother in them there pictures in that psychology book. It ain't so much from not knowin that causes trouble as it is knowin so much that ain't so. Supposedly it got back. The space monkey, not the mother. Getting a little sick of eating this here dry dog food, just about out of sugar and I've got no more reconstituted milk to dress it up. Yep, but I'm savin money — it's only costing me 25 cents a day for three daily servings. I've got to thank Cousin Alfred for introducing me to that Honorable Reverend Minister Bob guy from the Sword and the Covenant. Bob was right about survivin! Louis Willy had been on the dry dog food regimen for a while, but it was good to have such an expert and educated man like Reverend Bob reiterate. I get all the vitamins, minerals, proteins and carbohydrates from this here hundred pound sack of dry dog food as much as a ton of potatoes!

But he did tell me to keep in mind that dogs and cats don't have the same requirements for vitamin C as do us humans, that's why I got this here jar of vitamin C; I like aspirin too. Heard it's not even been invented yet in U-rup — with their socialist health care system where they are just a languishing in cots waiting for their bedpans to get changed… look at how healthy everybody is here in this bus… (he's tellin this to a French guy and his petite girlfriend who speaks no English — the French guy says they more resemble pre-diabetic, fattened cattle waiting for slaughter) It's all about the philosophical survival as the Reverend Bob tells me and you gots to keep alive with only one goal in mind: victory, moral victory! Be a spiritual warrior! Prepare ye! Victory is what Reverend Bob told me, and the victor will inherit whatever world is left after the Zombie Apocalypse and build a pure Christian society. That'll be somethin! And a bunch of wives to boot! O no that's the Mormons Louis remembers. Or is it them Hadji Muslim ragheads? This is your Paradise…

Louis Willy's imagination is lapsing through with the visionary dream of spiritual warfare Reverend Bob had transposed to him due to not being able to comprehend what exactly a pure Christian society was. It almost sounded social-listic. But Louis Willy had faith in the everlasting words of the Reverend Bob and he was glad to be of some assistance and personally deliver this here large box to some friend of the Reverend Bob's who would be waiting for him at the bus depot, a member of the Sword and Covenant and founder of the Goose Club, whatever that was. Louis Willy assumed it was some kind of hunting club; sportsmen and all. Louis Willy liked hunting. Yep, dry dog food make a most nourishing meal for a Christian soldier. Gee all them wives to make little white babies — (he guessed that was important) Louis Willy adjusted the cup to the athletic supporter he always wore — never knew when some crazy fucker might just jump out and try and kick a guy in the nuts.*

---

*   Louis Willy's practice in the art of num-chuks had been much more the reason for this peculiar habitude of wearing a cup than any threats of crazy fuckers jumping out to try and kick him in the nuts, knock himself right out, hittin his self in the head or the nuts. Sometimes, woke up in a woeful mess.

Yup, there he was, Reverend Bob's buddy, all dressed up in a suit and bow tie like them fine prim fellows back on the streets of Detroit sellin' Louis Willy them delicious sweet potato pies with that there newspaper The Final Call — from the Nation of Islam or somethin and the lost tribe of Shabazz with some scientist named Yakub 6000 years ago on the Greek island of Patmos — guess Islam started in Detroit, I dunno man — outer space, Louis Willy thought. The man's name was Adolf Mungu — very serious man and most abrupt with Louis Willy. Told Louis to call him in Seattle from a certain pay phone on Second and Union at a certain time in two days written on this card he handed him; gave him $500, told him there'd be another $500 for him if he called and followed the instructions. Mister Adolf Mungu took the package and left; on the card Adolf gave him some text read: The goyim are a flock of sheep, and we are the wolves. And you know what happens when the wolves get hold of the flock. — The Protocols of the Learned Elders of Zion.

"Huh? — don't know what that means," Louis ses to himself.

Walter has just gotten back from shooting with Mac out at a clear-cut near North Bend — they had had with them a trunk full o' guns. A quiet man named Hamid had joined them. Walter had barely shot more than a Red Ryder BB gun. It had been beaucoup fun — lots of bang-bang. Hamid and Mac had taken off in Western attire shirts and cowboy boots to do some two-steppin at the Little Red Hen, a honkey-tonk in the middle of hip Seattle. "Drink a little spirituous water. Get a little exercise and some squeeze, nice and warm — not like cold weights at the Y…" as Mac put it. Walter had joined him a few Tuesday nights and was quite impressed with Mac's country swing… as well as his baby-blue silk Carolina Tar heel jacket (the guy had more coats than anyone could imagine) — So Walter is perusing thru The Stranger; the local hip rag, reading the crime beat when his eyes happen to come across a little peccadillo about somebody he believes he had the sweet pleasure of having just met. The vignette headlined: Crazy Vietnam Vet — Chinatown Tuesday November 23 3:30 pm — A part-time day laborer who is obsessed with weapons and "lives in his Vietnam War past," was arrested for a weapons violations today. For months the man had been intimidating co-workers out of the Millionaire's Club, his place of employment, that one day he would snap and carry out a violent attack. He had recently come to work with a hand grenade and pulled the pin but then quickly replaced it. On another occasion, he showed his co-workers a photograph of himself with an assault rifle, which he explained was "fully automatic" and "illegal to own." This week he told another worker that he was practicing hard for a shooting competition the following weekend in San Francisco — he said he would be very depressed if he didn't win and might snap. When police learned of these threats, they got a warrant and entered his apartment at the Morrison Hotel and found it jam packed with grenades, guns, ammunition, martial arts weapons and knives. Police were initially unable to find suspect but eventually located him a few blocks away at Spin's Friendly Tavern. The Vietnam vet was arrested. When asked about the threats he made, he said he was only joking, and never intended to "shoot up the neighborhood."

Sounds just like that character Rusty, that Mac introduced me to over at Barney's Pawn Shop who we then went up to meet again at The Comet Tavern. It's got to be him — Chinatown, part-time laborer out of the Millionaire's Club, vet, some banter about "snapping" and then of course we all had to meander our way to the Dome Stadium Tavern after some pizza, to cool a few, a place chock full of a bunch of sunny-jims. Ah, these illustrious associates of Mac's just keep piling up in mounds. Seems Rusty knows Maurice. Funny little circle. Another evening. Guess we gonna play some pool... eight ball — corner pocket.

As the circle tightens, with darkness crawling along the pavement, they get in the car; Walter driving . The radio is on — something about — U.S. airstrikes. And Mac ses, "Doncha luv hearin that — U.S. airstrikes. It sounds so normal, kind of reassuring almost.

Just somewhere — Out There — there are U.S. airstrikes happenin; that's all we need to know. Keepin us safe. Pull over here."

So Walter winds up at the Comet Tavern and having a couple with Mac and Rusty — old dubious cohorts. The walls are covered everywhere with elaborate colorful graffiti; Ethel, the old barkeep is shouting out orders to the other bartenders, the old tan dingo dog with red kerchief on is at top of stairs sitting like a sage Egyptian sphinx observing and taking in everything, Ed Comet is at the end of the bar near one of the pool tables sayin to himself, "my peoples luvs me… and I luvs u people…" And Screamin' Jay Hawkins is wailin on the Mexican radio — "I Put a Spell on You!"

Rusty seemed to hold the old cohort sentiments nearer and dearer to him than Mac it appeared to Walter and first impressions are important. There was a lot of talk about people Walter did not know and places, dames, hotels, bars, ships and guns that Walter had barely or never heard of — Chu Lai, Pleiku, Dutch Harbor, The Elbow Room (in Dutch as well as Columbia City — Rainier Way) the F/V Golden Alaska, Hanoi Hannah, Plain Jane, the Ia Drang Valley, Barbara Stanwyck, the M/V Sally J, Happy Valley, benefits of the SKS rifle, the ship — The Eastern Wind, Kodiak Island, the Fabulous Rainbow, Yakutat, Plain of Jars, the Place Pigalle… and whatever happened to Yakima Canute? and whatever happened to Sean Flynn?… "and if we get rid of all the drunks — whose gonna do all the work?!" Rusty exasperates red-faced. Walter grabs a few peanuts and heads to the graffiti-laden men's room and looks up from the urinal and reads:

Bones

destroy the mind

destroy the memory

destroy the soul

inebriation is a rite of man

lose one's self   forget forget   forget

sleep

            wake up in the morning

ringing in the ears   moss on the eyes

bones and sinew   shake and clatter

Who am I?

It was all too much to file, but there was one very noteworthy bit of verbiage that Walter found special. "It was a little story, a true story, that once upon a time, this is no shit…" It was Rusty's story:

"It happened to me the other night at a bar… I was sitting there, havin a beer with this guy, I turned for just a moment and the guy is gone! Nothing but his baseball cap on the stool, his boots and the burning cigarette in the ash tray — I swear to God! Looked all around for him. Must've been that spontaneous combustion stuff goin around I figured. You just never know…"

As Mac just stares vacuously into the bar's mirror contemplatively finishing a cigarette, puts it out, stands up, shakes hand with Rusty and tells him, "Yeah, well fortune telling is for lunatics and old women. We'll be in contact with you later. C'mon Walter, let's go get some pizza at Piecora's, pick up some paint and hardware at Chubby and Tubby's for the future fireworks, do a little more Re-Search and then go make some shylock loans for some mon-nay." Walter slurps down his beer and sez to Rusty, "Nice to meet you," as he scuttles off behind Mac into the dark and cold night.

Mac turns to Walter and says, "Rusty did too much time in Graves Registration. Got stuck in the brig at Long Bihn for a while too, during the jail riots — known to the GIs as LBJ." Walter then notices Mac crossing himself — for not being very religious, Walter thinks; Mac's damn superstitious.

Crime is, by nature, a secretive thing…

✂

He is introduced by Mac to a large fit man with a bristly black beard and rather bristly short black hair and horned-rim glasses whose got on top of his left hand a tattoo of the Zig-Zag rollin' paper dude — kinda French looking, Quebecois... "Walter, this is Nitro. He's a recent graduate from the Monroe Reformatory." And on the sly Mac whispers to him about Nitro's habits of bundling people and taking them by their scientific necks in order to keep the complaints down as he goes thru their pockets upon darkened doorways. His occupation. "He's gonna ride with us. He's got some talents we could use."

Nitro gets right into his space and looks very intensely into Walter's eyes and shakes Walter's hand vigorously to the extent that it actually hurt Walter's hand. "Ow! Jeez-us!" Walter cries. Nitro ses nothing much but, "How do you do? Yew Ah-rish?" Dude's kind of East Coast with an undercurrent of physical menace. Got a head like a gasoline can and a nose that looks like it's been busted and reset by a plumber. He is dull of mind, blunt of spirit, numb of history. Eight miles of bad road. Perfect...

"No, no Walter here is of Viking stock, Nitro. Not an Irish Jew like you."

So they go a ridin on a quest for more incoherent vice. Walter drives. Nitro's in back. It's mostly quiet. They listen to 880 AM — "Music of Your Life" down kind of low — nice backdrop; a little Frank Sinatra, Bobby Darren, Ella Fitzgerald. All's pretty good 'cept for Nitro occasionally whackin his fist into his palm with an odd guttural grunt or two. Then Mac blurts out: "What do you think Nitro — black, white, Mexi or Jew?"

"I thinks Dixie tweekers..."

"Fuk! I should have hit the men's room... pull over to those ship containers... by them oil barrels."

"Just go up this way a few kliks," as Mac gives Walter directions to a certain locale over along the Duwammish River, south of Harbor Island and the shipping cranes. They pull up along near the

South Bridge by a one story Highway 99 low-rent kind of motel. The neon of the motel's marquee don't flash here no more. Permanently out. Mac tells Walter where to park so it's a straight shot out to the roadway and Lucille Street. Tells him to keep the car running. Walter has always been surprised at the juice the old green Ambassador's got. He does as he's told. Nitro and Mac move calmly, but swiftly towards a certain room and from there Walter's vision is somewhat blocked as to what transpires. Probably nothing, Walter's mind bullshits him. They are gone a while, maybe to just visit some old girlfriends. He hears a bit on the police scanner, but mostly he continues to listen to 880 AM — "Music of Your Life" with a little Bobby Vinton, some Andy Williams, Nat King Cole and then Perry Como starts singin a swell little song about Seattle. It's all very nice and pleasant. Walter's getting use to this — putting out his cigarette and watching the action on the street, he decides to roll another, making observations of the comings and goings. Walter has learned that Mac and Nitro were cellies back in Lompoc. A car load of Indians pulls up — Walter reads the bumper sticker: Proud to be a Ponca Indian. Walter contemplates like Russell Means says — Indian car, go far. Suddenly, Mac and Nitro are hurriedly upon the car and inside and Mac shouts, "Go!Go!Go! — C'mon!" for Walter has slipped into a reverie and rhythm to the night and the music and it takes him a moment to kick the auto into gear and a spedding off they make their getaway. Walter looks thru the rear view mirror and against the street lamps and fluorescent and neon lights of the motel he observes a number of silhouettes running in and out of the room. And he sees some smoke and fire.

Mac just says, "Nice work Nitro. That be a trifecta. Fuckin cholos." Mac pulls out some fat stacks and hands some to Nitro. Nitro, the ruffian grunts approvingly. The misfits head to the quiet streets of Georgetown, jammed between I-5 and just past Equinox Studios and north of the Boeing Airfield, to Jules Maes Saloon, amongst the ancient brick warehouses, near the old Rainier Brewery and the many ghosts, to have a few refreshing beverages to cap the late evening off to the music of their lives. And Walter contemplates Nitro's other tattoo, which is on his right forearm and is the Statue of Liberty with

a kerchief over her nose and mouth like a bandit or gangster holding a .45 automatic pistol rather than the torch with a visage of the
Virgin Mary as the base. Now that be a wild tattoo…

One night, Mac, Maurice and Walter head to Fremont for a
party to unveil the 17' high statue of Lenin (yes the V.I. Lenin —
this is no shit, like a true war story). They all pile in Maurice's little
VW bug and head towards the Tyrell's Dog Food plant along the
Lake Union Canal, but first they pick up Bill the Sculptor at the
Kalakala ferry boat (he's the night-watchman along with the ghosts).
The Kalakala Ferry was an aerodynamic space age sleek-looking giant
floating toaster that graced the Seattle shores thru the 50s and 60s
till it wound up grounded in Kodiak Island — Alaska, serving the
ignominious fate as a cannery. So this guy Bevis who was working as
a commercial fisherman saw it and decided it should be rehabilitated
to its past glory. He is also the owner who had built the Foundry for
metal bronze sculptors. So Bevis and some of his buddies borrow a
tug and very near catastrophically drag the listing, leaking Kalakala
back to its homeport of Seattle. Thus various welders, shipwright and
marine engineers donated their very skilled time to the rehabilitation
of the boat as well as many limited-skilled people volunteering to
chip paint and rust from the hull of the hulk. Thus Bill the Sculptor
had a home right on Lake Union with another alcoholic jarhead of
dubious distinction who couldn't join the merry crew cuz he was still
sleeping it off from the night before.

The entourage is a little early so they head up to the Triangle
Tavern where Bill has fabricated a custom metal outdoor-seating pe-
rimeter fence for the bar, but they are not allowed in because Bill has
been 86'd from the establishment. They grumble a bit about this,
sours their disposition, but Maurice says, "The party is probably getting going now — fuck this place. Let's go — Allez." They head on
back. The party is warming up. The wine is flowing, the kegs are
tapped, the band is having loud technical difficulties, molten metal
is getting cast as plumes of smoke waft high overhead along with the
clouds of ganja and tobacco. Bevis and a few of his Carhart-wearing
Comancheros are passing a whiskey bottle around. They have just
flown in from England where there had recently been an oil spill and

they had made molds for casting the dead oily birds on the beach as well as the dead fish and sea mammals. It is a specialty of Bevis — a statement, so to speak — sculpture of road kill. They flew off loaded on whiskey and wearing greasy Carharts and they arrived back a week later looking and loaded exactly in the same condition and manner — just a bit more sand in their hair and a bit more ripe. It was time to celebrate! Bevis donned on his American Indian buffalo head and carried his staff around like some kind of Comanche chief (Walter suspects the guy might be a bit delusional). The only real light in the cavernous concrete structure is coming from the band's stage lighting and the burning molten lava that is being poured. V.I. Lenin gazes sternly upon the bacchanalia, but Baudelaire is smiling somewhere… Walter has never been to the Foundry before and thought it was one of the coolest happenings he'd ever seen with the chicks a dancing a go-go. Walter notices Mac and his Fu Manchu mustache are doing some prime-time with vodka — clear spirits… Then some Gypsy Jokers who'd lost their way from the Fremont Tavern wandered in to the fiesta. They grin, they scowl. They scowl, they grin. Mac doesn't like the look of them. He prefers Bandittos. The party rages. Bevis is up on the mezzanine deck raising his staff to the East, to the West, to the South, to the North. One of the Gypsy Jokers tugs on a sweet young thang's hair as she dances to the beat. He swings her around. She pulls away; her eyes flash disdain and contempt. Mac leaps upon the biker and trips and flips him over his head and laid low the biker upon his back as Mac has broken the bottle of Stolichinaya and has it to the Joker's throat. Maurice grabs Mac's arm before he cuts. The hippy girl gets away. Fergie, a very large industrially forged fisherman/sculptor bear hugs the other biker crushing him… Maurice hisses, "Arret!" to Mac. They throw them out and take the boots to them a bit in a tidy little bundle. The band keeps playing, everybody keeps dancing — hardly anybody saw a thing. Like it didn't happen. Walter is astounded at the speed and adeptness. He is an observer. Maurice decides it is time to go. Bill the Sculptor is running around with his raspberry beret on and his pants down. He's doing ok so Maurice and Mac and Walter load up into the old VW bug. Mac is very drunk and raving incoherently while

Maurice is driving, making his way to I-5. Walter is in the backseat kind of exhilarated. Maurice says to Mac, "What the fuk are you doing? We got business to attend to. Hank is coming soon — you can't miss Uncle Henry coming to town. You could have taken care of that sans so much aplomb and drama." They are going fast south, down on Interstate 5. The little VW bug shakes and quakes, rattles and rolls down the asphalt/concrete corridor. Mac has by now gone from raving to utter rage and is damn near frothing at the mouth. There was war in his body. Maurice is speaking angrily in French smoking a Gaulois. Walter is buzzed out of his brain, agitated and excited by the alcohol and the little blow a woman generously bestowed upon him at the party. Surrounded by the tight quarters of this tinny capsule projecting thru time and space, and trapped, but exhilarated in the combustible atmosphere of anger and violence, almost believing that Mac is just foolin. Walter eggs Mac on and Mac is turning around screaming in fury like primal and Walter is catching glimpses of the look in Mac's eyes from the overpass bridge lights of Pike and Pine to realize too late — he is gone, the End... this is the Apocalypse... "We are already dead!" Bam! Mac smashes out the windshield of the VW whippin down the highway at 70 mph. The wind rushes in as Mac raves on, "Love is the only weapon! Bullshit! I got all kinds of weapons! I got dynamite! I got machine guns! Grenades! Got me a rocket-launcher! Bullshit! Love is the only weapon! I will fight! I will fight! The bullets scream to me from somewhere, they ain't never found a way to kill me!" Maurice is pissed, but remains pretty damn calm and says, "Look what the fuck you did, now you gotta fix my windshield." Walter pretty much shats himself. This evening, Mac has displayed a capacity for physical violence much out of Walter's realm of imagination. For the remainder of the windy drive, A3 continues on the stereo with the Most Reverend Dr. D. Wayne Love proposing a Hypo of Love. And Walter thought — the onliest way... being at peace.

They arrive back at the gallery. Maurice turns to Walter and casually says, "Mac's just got a little shell-shock. He'll be ok." A group has a craps game happening — "Snake eyes! Snake eyes! Roll seven! Be a natural! Box cars!"... A friendly game of poker and roulette ensues… Riz and Tamlin play some ping pong. While Zevon and Ted Joans compose poetry. KCMU with "Shake the Shack" a rockabilly venue is on the Mexican radio with some Knut Bell and Reverend Horton Heat a playin' as Kennedy with large scar across his forehead is twisting some neon telling tales of Spain and Algeria back when he was driving truck in the Franco/de Gaulle era and about chauffeuring John Lee Hooker and Muddy Waters around town, takin' em fishin with big fat blondes to Green Lake back in the Medicine Hat days; and partyin with the Hell's Angels for three days straight at Altamount, repeating in reverie: "it could be worse, it could be worse…" Kamau is shooting pool with Dready Anthony as Rolle, Jacque, Belmondo, Hamid, Major Leroy Capili (the Hawaiian lepruchaun) and the Rocket Metal boys from Oakland are gathered around the great round wooden table like a band of knights. The platoon of feringhee at the table all continue drinking, snorting and smoking; watching "Rocky and Bullwinkle" re-runs. Mac continues with blood-curdling howls of pain as if he was tied to the whippin post — agony, rage and terror, lurching about like a monkey-fanged demon, like a primordial Cro-Magnon caveman as was Walter by this point — nearly crawling like homo-sapian simian Neanderthal coming out of the Great Rift Valley having not quite figured out how to stand erect and wondering where is their prehensile tail. And Walter in quiet desperation looks into eyes of Mac's insanity and smashes a beer can with his forehead and then for a few moments a dull glimmer comes across Mac's eyes, he smiles cuz Walter gets it, he finally understands and he shouts out, "I love this guy! I love this guy! I give all my love! All my love! Pour La Legion!" and he falls forward, passing out in a blissful, heavenly sleep. A little rest for the wicked. When good things happen to bad people… Maurice shakes his head and goes back to the big table and Hamid hands him a translated letter he received from a cousin in Qatar: In accordance with God's will, we pronounce to all Muslims the following judgment — To kill the Americans and their Judeo-Crusader allies — civilians and military — is an individual duty incumbent upon every Muslim in all countries, in order to liberate the al-Aqsa Mosque and the Holy Mosque from their grip, so that their armies leave all the territory of Islam, defeated, broken, and unable to threaten any Muslim. This is in accordance with the words of God Almighty: Fight the idolaters at any time, if they first fight you; Fight them until there is no more persecution and until worship is devoted to God: Why should you not fight in God's cause and for those oppressed men, women, and children who cry out: Lord, rescue us from this town whose people are oppressors! By Your grace, give us a protector and a helper?! With God's permission we call on everyone who believes in God and wants reward to comply with His will to kill the Americans and seize their money wherever and whenever they find them. We also call on the religious scholars, their leaders, their youth, and their soldiers, to launch the raid on the soldiers of Satan, the Americans, and whichever devil's supporters are allied with them, to rout those behind them so that they will not forget it. All these American crimes and sins are a clear proclamation of war against God, his Messenger, and the Muslims. Religious scholars throughout Islamic history have agreed that jihad is an individual duty when an enemy attacks Muslim countries. Resist the New Rome — Depose the Tyrants — Go with the Winds of Faith Osama bin Laden — Maurice finishes reading and gruffly says to Hamid: "Sounds like a man we can do business with."

A few days later: the fuel pump was out in the Ambassador aka Green Hornet — so they pushed her into the loading bay at the gallery to work on her later. Mac shouts with joy, "Well, desperate situations call for desperate measures. We need to fire up the Norton!" The Norton had stood in one of the corners with a menagerie of carcasses and hulks of old motorcycles, truck engines and miscellaneous trannies. The old Norton was by far the most intact, the old Indian motorcycle had a ways to go. "Walker doesn't need to know if we borrow one of his motorcycles; 'course he's off filibustering in Nicaragua anyway…" So with a little mechanicking and close enough engineering; some starter fluid, baling wire and majica (magic) they (Mac) got the Norton to go. Walter did not know how to operate a motorcycle so Mac sans license was going to have to commandeer in their quest for scratch. So in order to obey the law and avoid Mom's House of Pain, they plopped upon Walter's head a motorcycle helmet — one of those fashionable Nazi style ones they found in one of the heaps. (It actually was a real Waffen SS helmet) And the only other thing they could find was a WWI leather flying helmet — with goggles, Mac put that on and away they went with Godspeed to joust with windmills and dragons, possibly all for the glory of Dulcinea. "Here you hold this package."

It was a bucket of Colonel Sanders Kentucky Fried Chicken. Walter thought it seemed rather heavy for a bucket of fried chicken.

"Hang on to it good. We need to get this to Josef. But first we need to find him. Jump on."

"Why are we delivering Kentucky Fried Chicken to Josef?"

"I know it should be Ezell's."

"But…"

"Look it's the law… cops can't dig in and check your food… besides you know, we're like Fed Ex or like uh, America… Democracy — We Deliver, just sometimes we do it with B-52s. Quit asking so many questions. You need to start relaxing, having some fun and enjoying life more. Walter — Behold a pale horse… It could be worse, it could be worse… It is all crystal clear…" Sometimes Mac repeats himself Walter notices.

It was sheer terror. The whole ride. Weaving in and out of the late afternoon downtown traffic, Walter would have soiled himself had he fortunately not expunged himself back at the gallery's WC. They happened to stop an 2nd and Union, not far from Bruno's Pizza and there was this hapless wino sitting on his haunches upon the sidewalk getting smacked up by a large young bare-chested thuggish fellow with pants riding jail-house low. The traffic had them stopped up next to them on the sidewalk as witnesses. So Mac yells at him, "Knock it off!" The thug stops beating the wino and looks up and calls Mac over. Mac pulls the motorcycle over and gets off as Walter does holding the bucket of chicken. Mac has removed the ridiculous goggles and like the wind has grabbed Walter's helmet and is holding it in his left hand. Mac eyes the slinking, skulking little sidekick sycophant of the thug-at-large having concerned of being shanked from behind. Then the thug waves him to come forward, "put down the helmet." Mac realizing there will be no peace in the valley until he puts the helmet down, does so as per requested. The two come forward. People are walking and driving all around, but most are not seeing any of this happening right before their midst — too busy texting. Walter, holding the KFC bucket, is standing there amazed at how Goliath here without shirt upon back doesn't seem the slightest bit cold and wondering what the fuck Mac of Mongol cast is going to do? The big guy can move and dances about in boxer mode and catches Mac one in the cheek and with that Mac let's go with a Cheyenne dog soldier war whoop and kicks the beast right in the jimmies which doubles Goliath over, thus Mac drives his elbows down upon bully's back; whackity-whack, crackity-crack: smack, smack and sez, slapping the young hateful prick's head into the sidewalk, "Don't pick on bums... no hard feelings." Blood flows slowly down the dirty sidewalk. "You know Walter — like I've said before, where there's love, there's Irish and where there's hate; there's more Irish. Let's git the fuk outta here before the cops arrive." One tall woman gave the fist-up power salute and said, "Right-on..." just like Angela Davis, as the pugilist and Sancho tool away upon steady steed of funky old motorcycle. She'd witnessed enough of the brutish behavior. Justice! Vigilante! Fear the mullet.

The subterraneans hit the Central, they hit Larry's Blues (the old blues speakeasy had definitely changed to a lot of thumping bass — boom, boom, boom-boom), the Double-Header, the Blue Moon, the Doghouse, the Zoo, the Skyway Park and Bowl Casino; they took the freight elevator up to the 211 Pool Hall amongst all the hustlers and grifters but all to no avail in their quest to finding Josef. "Let's head to 6th and River South to the Brothers of the Sun Motorcycle Club, Cat parties with those guys, maybe he knows of Josef's whereabouts and if no luck, then we'll go to Thompson's for another point of view." No, nothing, nada — Cat didn't know of the whereabouts of the dark prince Josef. It was a news black-out, as Walter examined the bullet perforated steel building serving as HQ for da club.

"I ain't bothering with Ozzie's... I'm hungry. Let's go to Ms. Helen's for some of that sweet potato pie and corn bread. Maybe they know where Josef is — fuckin doesn't answer his cell phone. man, it's time to gin-up, that chicken must be getting cold by now. Don't let it out of your sight. I'll practice some remote-viewing. You know American women are funny, but not in a ha-ha way… Why can't they be nice like us?" Walter had serious doubts about chicken being the contents of the Colonel Sander's bucket.

Ah yes, they enjoyed a fine quiet meal of soul food and the lovely, tall bespectacled waitress with an easy smile and pretty corn-rows, informed them that yes Josef had just been there and was on his way to the Elbow Room in Columbia City (not Dutch Harbor) Giving her a handsome tip for her welcomed tip, off they sped down Rainier to South Seattle. The mod squad arrive at the Elbow Room, just past Stalin's Barbershop across from Bob's Butcher Shop on the other side of Angie's Tavern, wading their way thru the diner heading to the back, up the stairs where the bar was located. Josef was inebriated and like some Wahhabi Arab sheik surrounded by a harem of lovelies. He seemed to sober up immediately with Mac's arrival and the Kentucky bucket of chicken. One of the harem said/asked Walter, "Are you a sociologist?" Walter who had a pretty good buzz on by now, shrugged cuz he really didn't know what to say — it was pretty damn dark in there, couldn't hardly see anybody in there. And boom! Poof! Walter looks around and notices 3/4s of the patrons of what had been a full bar had all of the sudden, out the side door and down the back alley; split — disappeared. Josef as well. It was most empty and in come the tall, rangy with black handle-barred mustache, wearing his black construction shit-kicker boots is the eagle-eyed Sheriff of Columbia City with his trusty, shaven-headed large-like black refrigerator of a partner. The police had arrived, doin the rounds, and besides the Korean bartender, some of Josef's harem, Mac and Walter and this little red-headed step-child, jaundiced-eyed whip of a hooker — the joint was empty. It was like that spontaneous combustion thing. Mac looks at the two peace officers right in the eye and gives them a little salute and they do likewise. Look around and leave. "Let's just say Walter that Phil and Bubba there along with Officer Muhammad and Officer Brown, do a munificent job keeping the Bloods and Crips in check — as much as possible, but still last week — uzis a-blazin, lots of bullets, down at Brighton

Beach Apartments with four dead… and foxy reporter Joyce Taylor running around — reporting. You should have seen it. Anyway, they do what they can; they are the law. Sometimes they need to make the law. Improv. Like sometimes you just got to have the guts to go and hit someone in the mouth — you know, cuz like they deserve it. Bully's only language — fear. These guys are a force to reckon with. Like leopards in the night, da gang unit. I'm beat, let's get back to HQ Manifesto. We'll hit Bob White's fruit/veggie stand — I feel like gettin me some Fay-go pop and then get some KC style BBQ at Jones off MLK and then Walter — we gonna get us some cake at Remo Borrachini's — cuz it's my birthday. Did I ever tell you about wrestling in the travelling ape show with the chimps: Butch, Joe and Congo — it was down south, of course, they just kicked our asses. Green Berets crying, screaming to get out… I lasted the longest. You know true war stories are never moral — it's just what we carry… Buddha will provide."

Bring out the balloons.

The large red neon sign blazes on the hill overlooking Rainier Way, offering reassurance that all is well by simply saying: WONDER BREAD.

Walter slowly shuffles over to get the mail — thinking of the Scottish girls he met a few nights before down in Pioneer Square at the Central Tavern. He let them share his room — they needed a place to stay, fresh off the Green Tortoise bus ride from San Francisco, but with the distraught girl sobbing herself to sleep, and her angry friend, it made the night's laundry awkward… Something for Mac from L. Ron Hubbard… Dianetics/Scientology — give Mac a free personality test — O my! There is one standard business-sized envelope addressed to a W. Curmudgeon in an almost child-like cursive scroll with no return address upon it. Walter opens it only to find three small folded up pieces of paper; on one side of one of the pieces in the same child-like scroll is simply written — We're still watching you from up here, closer than ever!

That was it — nothing more, nothing less, but on the inside of the three of the three small pieces of paper were these three individual maps, two that specifically laid out the whereabouts and cross streets of the gallery and where the gallery exactly set was an X with a red circle around it. The other little piece of paper's map was of the same 3 1/2 x 3 1/2 inches, but showed a larger geographical area that encompassed Interstate 5 and Interstate 90 and part of Lake Washington and part of Lake Union and Elliot Bay as well. Basically, a map of the main thoroughfares that led to the gallery. Walter could only guess who could it be from. He looks closely at the outside of the envelope to see where it had been mailed from and he could barely make out that it was from Santa Cruz, California. It freaks him out because no mail should have been reaching him at this address — not even from his mother.

Who sent it? The CIA, Louis Willy, the Hell's Angels, the Michoacán Cartel, maybe the Illuminati, or nebulous enemies of Andre? Who?! It was simply unnerving. His enemies are getting nearer. What Maurice always say? — do not confuse the map with the territory… In the back, somebody is playing on the pinball machine — the bells, whistles and noises do not help… Walter decides to take a valium or two, sits in the old-timey barbershop chair, gets out the binoculars, looks out the big plate windows and scopes out the action… keeping an eye on the dice games and addicts — quaking from the drugs the night before, vaguely recalling, trying to remember — did the cops show up at that party last night? He had stumbled and staggered into the smoky-layered gallery late that night… and there's Mac with red band around his head, Nambu and this group of hard-eyed Asian men he'd never seen before; probably Triad Chinese and Khmer Rouge around the big wooden table — were they really playing Russian roulette? He shuddered, shaking it off — probably just the drugs. The damage done. Maybe he should have taken a few less shrooms out of that McDonald's sack they were passing around at the party… He had drunk a lot of beer too. A crack-head woman squats and takes a pee right in the middle of the sidewalk. Walter puts down the binoculars. More noise please…

A week passes: The door bell rings like a 1930s telephone, Walter ambles his way across the gallery to the front door; a bouquet of flowers is sitting on the piss-stained, wino-shatted front stoop. He picks it up to find a little postcard addressed to him with a little note. It reads: I Know Where You Live — I Know Where You Are — You're Dead.

Walter shakes like Don Knots in "Mr. Chicken."

Mac arrives, sees that Walter is a racked with anxiety so declares it is time for a little recreation. Mac was a pretty good cook on the hot plate — did wondrous things with wok, squab and ramen, must have had something to do with his blue-eyed bamboo kid back in P.I. It ain't Coca Cola man, this guy cooked some rice. But what they needed sometimes were eggs. So they went out and got some. Mac liked to incorporate things — so this procurement of eggs had aspects of training and exercise involved, nutrition and cuisine as well as the making of money. Walter had been out on a few of these expeditions before. Walter served as an assistant and tender. And what all this entailed was Mac would scale the various brick warehouses, old concrete and steel bridges, and storage silos that abounded in old Seattle to collect the pigeon and seagull eggs to cook or to sell down in Chinatown as quail eggs. He'd sell them to Liem of Liem's Pet Shop for a bargain. Stealing the eggs from crows was exceptionally perilous, they would aggressively dive bomb in at him as he fended them off. He tended to leave the crows alone — said it was bad luck to steal from crows. Mac considered it all part of his American Warrior Free Fighting System training — looked like a real workout to Walter. Mac said sometimes he would have to practice astral projection to overcome the binds he would find himself in. It was excellent for keeping his SERE skills honed which Walter learned SERE meant: survival, evasion, resistance and escape — more pleasant poetic military haiku.

Sometimes ropes were employed, other times not. One time, as Walter was below on the railroad tracks, Mac had collected a dozen or so eggs and had reached the top of the bridge and the cops showed up and started running towards Mac. So Mac gave Walter the warning to run, and he rappelled down off the bridge making his escape, but was real pissed off about losing that good climbing rope. It was all good clean fun, so off they went; this time heading towards the West Seattle Bridge. It was very productive and unusually not very eventful, cops didn't chase them and nobody shot at them, no drama. Walter was amazed. But the evening would be different; Mac suggested they go to a reggae peace show at the Paramount Theatre. Cat-O-Nine was working security and they could get in for free by a side door. About five bands were scheduled with Lucky Dube headlining who was coming all the way from South Africa.

They dropped off the eggs and caught the short bus up towards Pike and walked the rest of the way. Cat was there in a side alley to greet them wearing a gray Persian lamb hat Mac said some Pashtun had given him in the guntown of Darra after a friendly game of buzkashi* in the Tribal Areas of the North-West Frontier Province of Pakistan. It was a nice hat Walter thought. So they get in, wafts of herb hover pleasantly as the beat goes on. Maybe the cosmos was trying to bring good vibes to the coming of the WTO. Mac and Walter leave Cat so he can get back to his job. They wander around enjoying the music, chilling out, gettin a little high. The bands come and the bands go. The Sharpshooters had just finished their set. Lucky Dube gets on stage with a retinue of beautiful women in traditional African garb, the men don guerilla ANC military attire. It's a great band! Walter goes up closer to the stage and the song "I Shot the Sheriff is playing" and bam! right in front of Walter some big-headed dude is dragging what looks like a chick by her brown hair and pummeling the hell out of her. Walter without thinking intervenes and then all hell breaks loose as the bull and his minions turn on Walter like a rabid pack. He's caught in the seats — got to get free of Big-Head. It's dark and everybody else is dark. Africans are flying everywhere — and then Walter is flying in the air above everybody's heads. He crash

---

*   buzkashi — a rough sport played in central Asia where they ride horseback like polo, but rather than use a ball — it is a poor goat.

lands and starts getting beat up again. But he fights back like Rocky Bleier, swinging wildy at the thugs, tryin to catch some teeth. The security are all wearing blue t-shirts and they were flying too along with the gang-bangers. Walter was getting smashed with several of the gang-bangers upon him; he was feeling like he was with the British Army at Rourke's Drift surrounded by the Zulus in the final stand when Mac and Cat pounce like jaguars and break some jaws. The band keeps playing, "but I did not kill the deputy…" one of the big blues gets a hold on Big-Head and that's when one of the Johnny gang-bangers with a pistol in his hand, puts it to Big Blue's head and all one hears is, "Gun!" and a fifteen foot radius miraculously opens up like the Red Sea as people duck for cover — with gun to his own head he let's Big-Head go and out the side exit door run the six gangstas with busted chops, loose teeth and sore heads, making their escape down the alley; homeys counting coup. Walter has blood running down from above his split left eye like a badge of courage; he is dazed. The lights turn on in the theatre. He staggers on up the aisle. Mac asks him if he's alright. Cat attends to some of security that took some licks. Officer Muhammad and Officer Baker of the Gang Unit show up, ask a few questions… Mac cleans Walter up a bit. Cat comes up and wraps a bandage around Walter's head and grins. Mac gives a little salute to Cat and the Gang Unit, takes Walter outside and flags a taxi and simply says, "Now that was exciting, Walter. Your Baptism of Fire. You now be a street-fightin man!"

Chapter Four

Please Kill Me

A psychotic is a guy who's just found out what's going on.

William Burroughs

Walter wanders past the entry and is immediately amazed at the mayhem that had been wreaked upon the gallery. Tables and couches are flipped over, garbage cans kicked over, but most noticeable is the broken crockery that has been flung all about; busted ceramic ash trays, plates and bowls of all different sizes and shapes and colors. Walter is indignant with rage that vandals have invaded the inner sanctum of the Manifesto Party HQ. Immediate paranoia follows the rational brain that this is an act of sabotage by the forces CIA! Or possibly the Knights of Templar. Walter is pissed as he scrambles about seeing what other damage has occurred and what papers are missing. Then he comes upon the letter that is posted atop the upside down empty coffee can serving as a candle holder in Walter's little rented studio — space/digs. It reads: Mr. Curmudgeon — received phone message — if you wish to respond, then please do so in writing. If so inclined, a chronological cause and effect approach to each issue is preferable. If necessary, I will respond in kind.

The scrawl was nearly illegible; then it dawned on him who had written it — Myron! Holy shit! Walter knew he had been acting erratic lately, occasionally Walter had seen him wearing a dress, but that wasn't that unusual in this reprobate neighborhood, but that's what everybody had said about him already and rumor had it that up in the Aleutians he declared one evening in the mess, that he'd run out of his "Meds" and the captain had choked on his turtle soup and had responded back in concerned inquiry, "Meds?!" and by about the third day after that revelation, not too far off Chignik, Myron was choppered off the ship in a straightjacket via sling and cable. But to think that he was the one running around amok thru the gallery tearing the place apart, destroying art — now this was too much! Walter with some trepidation went over to the other side of the building to Myron's crib over by the fish aquarium. The door was shut, Walter tapped on the door — gently, gently. He definitely could tell someone is on the other side for he could here the burbling and bubbling of bong and could see the smoke wafting out of an upper vent and smell that sweet pungent...

"Myron are you there?"

Then a shrill yelp let out, "Go away! Respond in writing!"

"Is it about the girl?"

There is a pause then the stereo is turned way up loud. The song is Aqua Lung by Jethro Tull. As Aqua Lung blares on loudly, Walter retreats to his area more confused than ever. He decides to take a shower wondering why he got that tattoo of the fierce tiger with the dagger thru its head. What a mistake. Up in Alaska, long ago. Should have gotten Tony the Tiger. He decides to take a long warm shower. He maintains his back to the wall so he is constantly facing towards the curtain — then he decides to turn his back. He didn't want to see it coming. It's kind of tough to really enjoy one's shower when you know there's a mad man loose in the house full of sharp utensils and general weapons. The scene from "Psycho" kept playing in Walter's head with that terrible high-anxiety theme music — that's why he had to turn his back. He just didn't want to see the big knife slashing down thru the plastic shower curtain and Myron's amphetamine-glazed eyes ogling on the other side of it. And that was part of the reason Walter took a long shower — if it was to be his last — let it be pleasant and most gratifying. He contemplated interfering with himself. Putting it in this perspective, Walter gave himself a most satisfying experience with the hot beads of water pelting his body, and fortunately the psycho never arrived via the shower curtain and by the end of his shower he had nearly completely forgotten about Myron. But when he grabs the YMCA towel and looks up and sees the shattered mirror; it brings him right back, all too much research... Walter tiptoes back to his area and finds this lengthy letter tacked onto the 4x4 post by an ice pick in front of his beaded entrance. It goes like this:

Mr. Walter Curmudgeon,

Attached is a letter I sent to my girlfriend Jolene. Please read this so that you might comprehend what your actions and Mac's have done to me.

When you arrived in here I offered you my friendship. I shared (very generously) many things with you and asked nothing in return, but offered and expected trust, respect and the mutual concern for well being that I shared with you. I introduced you to my friends, spoke highly of you, shared my thoughts and knowledge which I sincerely thought would benefit you. You in return invaded my privacy, betrayed my trust, didn't respect my personal property and acted without concern for my well being.

After having invaded my privacy and disrespected my personal property you then betrayed my trust by revealing a harmless personal fantasy to others and distorted a temporary state of mind and so damaged my reputation and future. Then you proceeded to torment me with constant innuendos. When I asked you to stop and limit the damage you had done. Next you insulted my intelligence and continued to betray my trust, invade my privacy, disrespect my property, reveal personal matters and engage in veiled Weimar discussions of same in my presence. You have continued to torment and damage my well being and sadly appear to derive great sadistic pleasure from doing so! You have caused me indescribable pain and slowed down my efforts to overcome past difficulties, their effects, and begin to fully enjoy life.

What kind of human being are you? You claim to act and people believe that YOU ARE the kind of person that would never harm or think ill of another human being.

I have tried to refrain from acting upon my feelings for subjecting you to an equitable retribution. I have no doubt that I would be completely justified! I sincerely hope that you think about what you have done and will choose to do next.

Myron X

That was the end of that letter — then along with that Myron for some perverse reason incomprehensible to Walter attached a copy of a letter he had written to his girlfriend Jolene. The whole thing was stranger than fiction, stranger than Payton Place and was only going to get worse as far as Walter could tell. So that's why he runs around breaking his own pottery — he hardly mentions Mac; Mac's the one who sets the little booby traps for him. Ah, might as well get on to the next letter to get a few more pieces of the puzzle of the mental fragmentation.

Here it goes:

Dear Jolene,

It's not easy for me to deal with an express my emotions regarding some of the experiences I have been through, both recently, up in Alaska and over the last few years. However, for both our sakes I must stop avoiding and no matter how unpleasant — fully deal with them. Hopefully, you might feel better if you knew more about what has affected how I act and feel. I didn't fully face the charges made by Mac and Siouxie that you were stealing from me. I cared enough and could reasonably cope with telling you about it. Also, I accepted your word on the matter and recognized that I should have defended you stronger, especially when considering their motives for doing this. Unfortunately, as more Mac and Siouxie accusations continued along with negative comments from others about your past and their opinion that you were just using me for drugs etc... I found it harder to deal with and didn't.

To compound things, something quite valuable, was stolen during this time. I can easily picture myself getting very pissed off and hurt if I was in your position. Without doubt I would consider many possible actions, which if not justified would normally never cross my mind. Especially, if compounded by hearing rumors about me, and being subjected to the effects of my self-conscious avoidance of them. I sensed that some people including my so called friends had never cared enough to find out the full truth from me and were continuing to spread false rumors about me. When I first sensed this was going on I should have dealt with it. Instead, I let it back a self-consciousness that overwhelmed everything else. Unfortunately from the past nightmares and pain from fighting rumors I wasn't ready emotionally to cope with it. It had appeared that once again what had all started many years ago might snowball into another all consuming nightmare. Although damaged from my failure to confront these problems sooner, I am going to try repairing as much as possible, and will not allow it to overwhelm and destroy me this time. To start, I'll share what has brought this all about. The first rumor started when an ex-roommate got arrested. Somehow the idea that I had set him up with the undercover narc went around. This was despite the fact that my ex-roommate knew and would tell anyone who asked that I never met the narc, nor was in anyway whatsoever aware or involved with what happened to him. As a result I was set up, attacked, mugged and robbed as well as asked to leave parties. The psychological paranoia and self-consciousness started then. This first rumor was not believed by any of my friends and easy to disprove with anyone who would listen.

However, the rumor was so widespread that there are still many people who didn't know me that continue to believe what was said. To this day, I still have to watch out where I go in Capitol Hill because so many idiots and low-lifes have never heard the truth. It's been hard to prove my innocence before being threatened or experiencing the unnerving effect of these people spreading the rumors to everyone they come in contact with. Over the next few years I became more self-conscious, less outgoing, bitter and started putting up a violent vindictive — don't fuck with me image to shield me from possible attacks. Next, a friend of mine had a little brother who found it amusing to tell his sister-in-law that my girlfriend Betty was missing and I had dropped out of sight and the police were looking for me. Incredibly because of his straight-faced approach, current news stories about some murders and my constant violent joking (intended to create protective fear) she believed him. Of course then she told others. Fortunately this time I found out in time to stop it effectively. The next afternoon, I stopped by a friend's house and his mother who had always liked me reacted very nervous and told me to go away. I knew she had some alcohol/drug and emotional problems and so assumed that she was just going through a rough time. Luckily, I then went over to a friend's wife for a haircut appointment. When I got there she seemed real nervous and frightened. It dawned on me that these were two very odd reactions on a row, so I told her about my friend's mom's reaction. She seemed puzzled and asked if I knew what was going on and if Betty had been found. When I explained that I didn't and had just had lunch with Betty she told me what her little brother-in-law had said. We called Betty and everyone though a little embarrassed laughed and it was all over. Most important, but already too late I recognized the damage my violent image and shield had done to my reputation and character. I began to tone it down and was having great success. It was then only minor effects from the narc rumor I suffered. I was going to junior college, working on the docks at Sun-Mar and Coastal Shipping, had plenty of friends, normal amount of girlfriends, confident and secure with life and the future to come. (Walter reads on more diligently and amazed — straight out of Dostoyevsky — Man is bound to lie about himself — Crime and Punishment)

Then out of the blue came a devastating real life night-mare. Someone started a rumor that I was a closet queen sexually. Ironically, it was all started because a guy was jealous that a young girl chose to go out with me rather than him. I laughed it off at first, since everyone assured me not to worry because it was obviously ridiculous and nobody would believe it. All's well that ends well right? WRONG! Soon I got reports that people were saying that I was offering a reward to find out the source, and would no doubt kill whoever did it. About the same time some-one started making obscene phone calls late at night and sending me used pornographic magazines with names like Honcho. I was annoyed and amused at the same time. Annoyed that someone would pull pranks like this. But also amused at how stupid they were, because sev-eral things made it obvious who was behind it. Unfortunately, I saw little harm in it all and assumed it would go away. Unknown and not foreseen by me the rumor continued to spread like a contagion and because of its nature and people's fear of my violent vindictive image, nobody told me about; it had grown beyond my belief. Then I found that when I fought it, my efforts actually did more to fuel the fire than to put it out. Everywhere I went people would at first like me and want to be my friend as I had always enjoyed, then someone would run into someone who heard the rumor and it would spread like the plague. People would avoid and distance themselves from me. Suddenly young ladies who had been very responsive would politely turn down or cancel our dates. I might then get upset and throw a fit which would only strengthen their suspicions — it would come out with subtle innuendo, a nod, a raised eyebrow or the like, then their suspicions would turn to unquestionable fact in their minds. Who I thought were my friends, began to distance themselves and join in the backstabbing of my character and reputation. Only one person cared enough to come to me with what they heard instead of jumping to conclusions. The rest acted without any respect, concern or consideration for the devastating results their actions could have upon the life of an innocent and loyal friend. Then after I was so deeply hurt that I started to withdraw from every part of what had been an enjoyable and promising life. Progressively, I became more self-destructive. Drugs, alcohol, dropped out of school, took lengthy time off on workman's compensation claims, drunk driving arrests, legal problems, financial ruin, destroyed all my pottery, allowed my health and appearance to deteriorate and eventually started to doubt myself; lose hold of reality and escape into a fantasy creating plans for becoming all the things I had been branded out of spite and contempt for everyone's injustice. (Walter keeps on reading even more diligently and more amazed, German Romanticism gone awry and amok again)

Fortunately, something deep inside me must have prevented me from striking back at everyone out of spite. (Yeah like maybe you'd get your ass kicked Walter says aloud "a bam-bam, bambam, I want to be sedated... gimme-gimme shock treatment... gimme-gimme shock treatment" as a little Ramones drums in Walt's head) Perhaps because my friends didn't see that they were wrong and sadly could not possibly have understood the impact to my life; nor could I abandon my lifelong values by becoming something I was not, despite a strong urge for spiteful revenge. (O brother — please... turn up the violin music — o the calumny! he's more a victim of the misunderstanding of others than I am: a day will come when a guy can't even pull on his pud in the privacy of his own Audi without some drone with a camera buzzing around sending him a ticket in the mail and requiring him to register as a sex offender — Brazil-like, Orwellian collateral damage: Walter digresses — sometimes the light don't shine) I had been through too much to be surprised when I started getting propositioned by friends, acquaintances, and strangers coming out of the closet because they heard the rumors. It was amazing to see the expressions of shock and terror of having exposed themselves, when I told them in no uncertain terms that I had never done anything like that, wasn't going to and never would. (Except if you were stuck in a Turkish prison singing The Song of the Turkish Damned Walter ad-libbed, attempting to deconstruct)

Eventually, after several failures to turn things around I hit bottom. It seemed as though I could never overcome this nightmare. The only choice I had seemed to be resigning as in a hopeless game of chess. Incredibly, despite consuming what are normally lethal amounts of cocaine, almost everyday, sometimes around the clock, I couldn't have a heart attack even after two months of what was suppose to be my secret personal last hurrah. Then something inside me came alive and gave me the will to try salvaging and regaining what had been my very special enjoyment of life and people. (Touched by an angel obviously — this place is just a hotbed for mental health Walter surmises) It's been quite an experience to climb up from where I cannot believe exists anything lower. (Believe brother... believe, you want horror — see Messieur Maurice prancing around first thing in the morning in his French thong and espadrilles gingerly sipping on his coffee splashing it with un petit Courvosier — That's horror)

When I met you I had come a long way from the bottom, but as I do today still had some distance to go, but finally was seeing the light at the end of the tunnel. It's amazing when considering the unique circumstances which brought us together, how I shared with you was the best thing that happened to me in many moons... blah... blah... blah.... from having been hurt by so many people. I'm sincerely in the human race blah... blah... blah... hoped... honestly... truth... learning... realistic... unfortunate... relationship... fair chance... any unpleasant feelings... paths... victim... choices... cutting your losses... Thanks for the good things you shared with me. I wish the very best of success and luck with finding everything you need in life.

Warmest Regards,

Myron X.

Now the only question was what was the point to having left this poignant document for Walter to peruse thru? A cry for help... Walter scratched his head most uncomfortably on this question and found all possible conclusions quite disconcerting — obviously his serotonin and dopamine levels are very jumbled. Better get a hold of Dr. Cuka. What did Mac say about Myron X — "Myron X fucks things up; cuz that's what he does." Maybe this is his way of making a pass at me… one just never knows. Indeed.

Walter then happenchance comes upon a book on narcissism and it reads: 10 signs that you are dealing with a narcissist. Walter pulls out a pen — 1) conversation hoarder (Walter went; check) 2) conversation interrupter (check) 3) rule breaker (check) 4) boundary violator (check) 5) false image projection (check) 6) entitlement (check) 7) charmer (no check on that one Walter thought) 8) grandiose personality (check) 9) negative emotions (check) 10) manipulation: use others as extension of Self. With that Walter concluded with all those checks Myron X just hits it out of the park as a raging narcissist with beaucoup borderline personality issues. Better put the book down now… Say no more, say no more… He goes over to the aquarium to feed the goldfish — and contemplates flying with koi. Then Walter decides maybe he just ought to meander over towards the Progressive Missionary Baptist Church at 14th Street to see how his buddies the white punks on dope from the punk band DSML were doing at their practice session. Maybe Little Ken isn't nodding out — poor little junky. As he leaves the premises, he observes Maurice and Mac in full theatrically flamboyant white Olympian regalia fencing on the street, back and forth with Maurice yelling: "Tonue Combat! Tonue Combat! Tonue Combat! React! React! React! — Attaque! Attaque! Attaque! Riposte!" Keep your distance in sword fighting and paintings. Walter recalls Maurice mentioning something of being a pentathlete for the Belgian National Team and he was beginning to think he'd seen it all, but he had not even come close. There would eventually be exhibits of Flamenco dancing with beautiful Spanish guapas by Maurice and Mac upon the streets of Seattle in front of the gallery. Insane as it ever was… insane as it ever was; his mind careens.

Chapter Five

Front Row, Second to the Left, Sharp Teeth

It is not necessary to censor the news. It's sufficient to delay it until it no longer matters.

Napoleon

Walter punched the clock arriving quite late at the office — a sub-manager was there to greet him at his pod as they called the office cubicles at Trimsetter Corporation.

"You're late and costing the team valuable points — points! points! I'm writing you up again Curmudgeon. Third time this month."

Walter replied in a sardonic monotone, "Sorry Mr. Radke — the vicissitudes of modern life, it won't happen again." Eyebrows raised with that response, Radke walked on, perplexed — what does he mean? Trimsetter Corporation had awards every month from "Most Helpful and Friendly Award" to the "Enthusiasm Award" to "Most Improved" to the old reliable — "Employee of the Month" and every month in the Trimsetter Times it would come out nation wide for everyone to read who had access to this publication. It was all part of the culture of working at Trimsetter. They had regional breakdowns like baseball statistics with everything from different divisions (American vs. National) to stats on rookie performers — sales, installations, telemarketing, collections, attendance, canvassing, and quality control — for example. Since sub-manager Radke's pod wasn't quite keeping pace in collections with the rest of Trimsetter's collection's departments (fifth place out of seven); Radke was going for the attendance award which would garner him a fabulous! amazing! breathtaking! four day trip to Paradise Island on the luxury Carnival cruise ship — the Love Boat along with three hundred other maximal production/top performer Trimsetter employees and their spouses. Walter was "letting down the team" as Radke like to put it, but Walter knew how bad Radke wanted to win that trip to the Bahamas and get his picture taken for the Trimsetter Times. Walter wanted to throw in his shoes and sabotage the entire process for Radke. Passive/aggressive Walter couldn't help it; besides that, he was just a temp — no stock options or insurance or 401k for Walter — why should he give a damn? And then he recalled what the sage Mac had said to him, "If you screw up; first, you deny it — second, you blame somebody else — and third, if you're just totally busted — you just put your hands in the air and say, 'Sometimes I just don't know what the fuck I'm doing!' It's what everybody does anyway — really."

Walter looked at the sheet posted on the latest up to date numbers. We were way behind in the Federal Division in collection dollars, but "we" had a fighting chance in attendance except for the Sioux Falls and Cincinnati offices that had nearly impeccable records — on time, never a sick day amongst any of the co-workers, just phenomenal! Walter found it hard to believe and doubted the polls. It was all very confounding to him how excited everybody was around here all the time. And then Walter thought back to junior high — how we were all getting along just fine, blacks and whites, till that show "Roots" came on — that's when the riots broke out. Looking back he didn't really blame his buddies for beatin on him. Piss off anybody to find out all our patriarchal TV stars like Pa Walton, Ed Asner and Lorne Greene were nothing but a bunch of sadistic, serial rapists. And he still wound up getting bussed... People get excited.

Walter went down to sit at his office (in his cubicle feeding station) He added the nondairy creamer to the Styrofoam cup filled with black coffee — powder. He began reading the Trimsetter Times just to get a pulse on what was happening — the heart beat of the company kind of stuff. It was required reading and the company policy that the first five minutes of the day to be designated to reading the company paper to learn and understand the Concern's World View. Work on that institutional memory. The script went on about how well the firm was doing, how the division standings were going for this fall's top telemarketing performers as well as top dieting instructors. Walter read up on how the aluminum siding conference champs in Oklahoma City are doing. Points, points, points — on time etc. Walter did his best to fight off these paragons of promptness and cleanliness. Since arriving, he was always getting it for the lack of order about his desk cubicle — empty ho-ho wrappers and the like. It was only a matter of time. Walter read on: how the "B" conference was doing in the American Division and how about those Wichita Prairie Pounders and who is going to win the Battle of/ for Disney? — (Walter knows that mouse is evil) — all team players here, it made Walter's heart proud like soaring eagle just to be a part of this well-oiled machine. To wrap up his required reading Walter read the little pep talk by the chairman of the board about how the whole company was like family and how the wives were the backbone of the veteran sales reps… (Walter wonders what decade are we in — is it the Mad-Men years?)… he reads the time tables and schedules for the mandatory management seminars and drug testing and last, but not least, a touching story about thirty year milestone with the company for manufacturing vice president Layne Wayne. Layne Wayne had been working at Trimsetter Corporation before Walter's first kiss playin spin the bottle; 'bout the time of the Fall of Saigon with the helicopters getting dumped off the aircraft carriers and the last desperate flight off the embassy rooftop… That realization put things a little more in perspective for Walter. Nothing but fat smiles in the photo ops and a quote from Layne Wayne how Trimsetter is truly considered home. Layne Wayne had started out as a dieting instructor at the Sacramento office before he wound up at the company headquarters in Indianapolis. There were a few photos of him in the 70s with sideburns, Tom Selleck mustache and a gold chain hanging off his chest — he must have still been a diet instructor in that shot. Walter realizes that if he plays his cards right — he could be that guy! But Walter's quest for consciousness expansion keeps telling him — "Don't be that guy, don't be that guy."

Walter then works on the word scramble on company time; they were suppose to do it on their free time, but Walter couldn't help himself. He was addicted to word scrambles, puzzles and Sudoku, but he was having a hard time with this one. Finding the words: delinquency, collections, missing docs... check-o-matic, default, lien, Equifax, and reject. He finally had to quit, it just wasn't worth it — it was too hard, plus as Walter looked up at the clock and realized an hour and fifteen minutes had passed from the requisite five minutes, he needed to do something else. He quickly put the corporate newspaper down and started shuffling thru papers. One he noticed happened to be from Arkansas. Texarkana, Arkansas. It was actually addressed to Walter's cubicle partner BJ Bittner, but he was out on the repo of somebody's Monte Carlo as a "volunteer" (a nice word for fool as far as Walter could tell) with the so-called "special forces" of the Trimsetter's Collection Department. These "special forces" usually came from the sky out of nowhere in black helicopters. Occasionally requesting the voluntary assistance of the various desk jockeys at collections. It was big points for those who volunteered and came back, but some never came back, or so Walter was told. The request came in yesterday for one backup; BJ beings a young Turk company-man kind of trooper, as well as being a reserve in the Washington State Guard with a young pregnant wife felt the need to perform, get in on the action, make a name for himself, earn a few extra bucks, bust some chops etc... so he volunteered to go out on repo duty; for a fist full of dollars and a gold star from the company. Walter tried to dissuade him telling him, "Those guys are nuts!" But BJ, bein from Texas (our favorite foreign country) wanted to be the man; anyway, Walter hoped BJ was ok.

Walter opened the letter. As aforementioned it was from Arkansas — Texarkana Arkansas from a Bertha Little of 222 Izard Street (another letter from Arkansas) It was the original Trimsetter Collections form letter addressing the delinquency of Bertha's account and current balance of $12,782.59 which was way past due and now accumulating at Jimmy Carter interest of 28%.

Attention Miss Bertha Little account #557-3259lpq-009: We've sent you notices, letters and tried via telephone. In the face of all this, you seem to be taking a "I care less" attitude. We care. And you should care... 1. About the fact changes are being added to the amount which you now owe, (to which on the side of the form letter Bertha made handwritten addendums — "i don't owe you nuthin") and 2. About the fact that your credit score is suffering. When we approved you credit, we cared about your need and you cared about your responsibility for repaying your account. I can see no reason why your attitude should have changed — (i don't have an account with you and you know that) We haven't. A brief talk with me today could straighten this matter out to everyone's satisfaction. DON'T DELAY — TELEPHONE TODAY!!!

Sincerely,

BJ Bittner

Account manager

(Mr. Manager why do you keep wanting muny from me you no i don't own u nuthin why you keep botherin me don't that bother you? u are unfair if i get another letter from you i am call a lawsuit or call Oprah. Don't write me or call me u know you never put that siding around my house)

Well, it's a tough situation Walter figured knowing the tactics employed by the Trimsetter Corporation in order to increase volume — strong arm methods and extortion-like means led to the greater profits, it was just that simple — the poor, the weak, the stupid, the old, the uneducated and the crippled were to be preyed upon. It was Hobbesian dystopia — the simple brutish Law of Nature, an edict, the strongest shall survive, dog eat dog, those who cannot adapt perish. Darwinian — the institutional memory was honed to a very high degree along this philosophy at Trimsetter Corporation. And Walter realized that whether Bertha Little ever had her house sided or not was irrelevant at this stage since it had gone to collections — there would be only one final and eventual outcome — Bertha Little was going to get fucked and there wasn't a damn thing she could do about it. Poor Bertha, Walter thought, poor all the poor people who fall prey to Trimsetter Corporation's diet and window programs. Chow for the feed line. Trimsetter was making a fortune in piastres.

"Hey Walt, how's it going buddy?" a friendly chipper voice came from behind the corduroy maroon partition and a beaming face leered over.

"Oh hi Chuck," Walter responded to the assistant assistant manager, (lots of titles at the Big Trim) Chuck Anthony just a little over a year on the job and just tearing them up and knocking them dead. Before Chuck had started his career at Trimsetter he had been in the Air Force. He had perfect teeth.

"Hey Walt buddy, you mind if I borrow BJ's phone for a few minutes? The maintenance crew is over at my work station and you know how those animals are to be around with…" nod, nod, wink, wink. "I just can't focus and concentrate on the job I'm here to do… You don't mind — do you?" Chuck confidently said smiling with his loud white pearly perfectly sharp teeth.

"Oh sure Chuck — anything to be of some assistance."

"Attaboy Walt — team player." With Chuck giving Walter a few faint jabs… Walter's boxing prowess is lacking.

Walter decides he'd better kick it in gear and really act like he's doing something as Chuck sits at BJ's desk and picks up the phone. Walter starts sifting thru the paperwork and comes across Policy and Procedure for Emergency Plans Manuel for Bomb Threats. Walter reads: Bomb threat check list.

"Why should today be any different? You need to have him give a call." As Walter overhears parts of Chuck's inner dialogue with the phone, Walter continues his work reading... When a bomb threat is received, document all the information and prolong the conversation as long as possible. Listen for background sounds. (Walter thought this is all wrong to begin with — do the right thing — scream BOMB! and hightail it out of the building as quick as possible)

"I'm looking for Sally Redding... that's her extension?"

Questions to ask:

"I was wondering if Ernest was in today? Housekeeping please. What can I do for you?"

When is the bomb going to explode?

"That will be on the pay sheet tomorrow. The last call gave me an asthma attack and I don't have any money to buy medicine — I see. Can you take a number for me?"

Where is the bomb located?

"And what is your name?"

What kind of bomb is it?

"Alright it's not my job to harass you, it's my job to make you pay your bill!"

What does the bomb look like?

"See I'm trying to help you with an interest payment — can you borrow the money?"

What will cause the bomb to explode?

"Is your mortgage up to date? How many Western Unions have you got? Anybody got a rubber band? Got a pencil handy, Walt?"

Walter hands Chuck a pencil and some rubber bands, and keeps reading: Who placed the bomb? Did you place the bomb?

"If I go too fast just tell me... take your time, that's fine."

Why did you place the bomb?

"And you are aware of our lien?... it's free advice."

Exact wording of the threat?

"That will come to $553.63. Is this their daughter? Oh you listen!… yeah you call your attorney and tell him that you don't pay your bills!"

Information about the caller's voice (check all that apply)

"I don't care how you get here — strap a mattress on your back!"

male female adult child

"Stop speaking for a moment!"

loud soft fast slow

"Time to get out of bed dude!"

local foreign

"In other words you are him, you just don't want to admit it…"

high deep calm angry

"How are you going to make a payment by the end of the month — the end of the month is TODAY!"

excited emotional drunk irrational

"Everything on your application is a lie!"

laughing stutter slurred raspy disguised other

"Go wake them up! Hey borrow a pair of shoes, hitch a ride into town and get down to that Western Union pronto!"

information about background noises (check any and all that may apply)

"Read our contract! You are in default! We're done doing our business — I'll see you in court!"

traffic airplanes music voices quiet office

I'll have a realtor out there this afternoon to take some pictures of our house! What size van do you need? Get out of my house!"

crockery PA systems motors animals machinery static

"You want to know what I'm going to do — read your contract! You should be ashamed of yourself — you're a grown man!"

house noises street noises other

"Do you need some boxes? Go pick up some cans! You can't pay your bills, but you can afford a lawyer…"

Remarks — name of person receiving the call, extension number receiving the call. Time call was received — AM/PM Date

"Thanks for your time," Click. Chuck hangs up the phone… feeling good, doing a few shadow boxing moves, he tags Walter a couple of times as Walter, with a stupid grin on his face, tries to pathetically deflect a few of the blows. He realizes he has no idea why he is grinning, but he believes it is probably just his survivor instinct kickin in to appease Chuck's alpha-dog bully id of ego. He cajoles Chuck with an, "Attaboy sport — way to go!"

"These people — they are such idiots! Gawd I love this job! The people — they are so Stupid! It's be-yooti-ful! It's the American Way — baby ye-ah! — Ah Walter don't you see, like our legal system it just comes to a matter of the smart people processing the dumb people, the smart people processing the dumb people… and on and on… It's fucking wonderful! Gawd what a kick-ass morning! I'm going to take a break and have a smoke — care to join me?" Chuck's just rushing.

"Gee Chuck, I've got a lot of work to get done otherwise I'd love to."

"Hey thanks for letting me use BJ's phone."

"Oh sure, anytime."

As Chuck saunters off to have a smoke, eyeing the latest temp women, Walter casually rolls back his chair to BJ's file cabinet and takes out Bertha Little's file, leafs thru it and deftly shreds it up with a handy scissors and with great stealth drops the contents into the waste basket, slapping his hands together as in a cleaning gesture just as Mr. Radke pounces upon Walter's station to shriek at him, "Why haven't you made any calls yet?! We've been monitoring your phone and you haven't made any — why not?"

"I was using BJ's, my phone jack's broken — I got the maintenance guys to fix it, if you examine your records, BJ's phone has been busy all morning. My partner BJ's out on repo. And now I've got a lot of paperwork to get done today."

"Hrrrumph…" Mr. Radke went off in a hoot.

Whooh! that was close, all part of the controlled-addictive technology… Oh Christ! here comes that new temp chick Jane with the brown moppet dreadlocks like the snakes from the Gorgon and with those John Lennon glasses; he turns to stone. She's got it for him. Walter could tell. Walter had let slip out a couple of suspect political remarks and ever since then… sexual tension. Heard she had lived in a tree in northern California. Maybe it was Oregon. He'd also spied Jane and her friend Femka coming out of the Socialist Workers Party's HQ at the Freeway Hall off Rainier in Hillman City as well as catching her reading and drinking tea at the anarcho-hippy Rainbow/Burning Man Gathering co-op Morningtown Café; but unbeknownst to Walter she had spotted him entering an "adult entertainment center" — but at least it was a strip joint owned and run by women, part of the feminista liberation theology. Love is a rose… So as Jane wags by Walter she surreptitiously drops Walter a note. Walter fumbles with it after he recovers from the sheer amazement to his addiction Jane. He opens it up like his own little magical kingdom and all it says is: "Henry Kissinger is coming to town for the WTO" — That was it?! That's it?! Well, well, well… she is in the Socialist Workers Party… what could the seditious bitch be up to Walter wondered? Their stern eyes meet. The Jezebel turns to enter another quadrant of the office. Walter decides he must get back to work and start looking busy. He decides to do an inventory of what contents are in his desk. He writes in his notebook:

Desk Inventory —

Upper Left Drawer:

Box of pay statements. Western Union stick-ums. Message pad. Trimsetter anniversary card. Box of envelopes (plain, Trimsetter logo) credit card forms. Copy of chapter about Jesuits from a book about secret societies. 2 box staples. Whiteout. Black pocket comb. 2 orange highlighters. 2 blue highlighters. Little white plastic skeletons (made in China). 12 certified mail slips. nickel 1972. 2 alcohol free resolution multi-purpose towelletes. 2 rubber bands. 1 Papermate blue medium point pen. 1 Papermate black fine point pen. 1 Bic black fine point pen. 1 Bic blue medium point pen with chewed end and no cap. One screw. 1 small box of Trimsetter diet pills. Chicago Cubs pencil. University of Oregon pencil. Indianapolis Motor Speedway pencil. A month to month inventory of the money Walter has collected up to now. 1 series of 20 cent stamps (Old Glory). A bunch of paper clips. Small cardboard box with a lot crap in it, some of which aforementioned.

Left Middle:

1997-1998 Seattle phonebook (U.S. West). 1 plastic spoon. 1 fork. 3 Quaker peanut butter and chocolate chip granola bars. Baggie with Dorito chip detritus. small red plastic plate. 1995 directory of member agencies of National Foundation for Consumer Credit. Microfilm order forms. Military Book CNb catalogue and order form. 2 BNG Music Service catalogue and order forms. List of Trimsetter offices. List of status codes. List of Federal Diversified Services employees.

Lower Left:

Legal forms. 2 Hello Direct headsets. Booklet on Law on how to use your Rolm Telephone System. canvas bag another headset comes in. CBR order forms. Copies of all collection letters. Bankruptcy forms (Chapter 7, Chapter 13, reaffirmation). Voucher requisitions. Copy of bonus plan 9s0. Fax cover sheets. Pay sheets. Release requests. Dead File forms. Skip sheets. Real estate worksheets. CBR universal data form. 401 K retirement form. Probate worksheet. CBR subscriber codes. Trimsetter stationary reactivate sheets. Settlement authorizations. Job description questionnaire. Trimsetter Corporate Communications chain-booklet. 3 pages of collection strategies. Copied article called "Love Hurts" about sexual injuries. 2 daily work schedules. List of legal queues. Judgment expiration log. Paid — by accounting codes. All my old pay logs. Aug 14th memo from Corporate Attorney regarding office. FDS customer survey. Faxed of Agreement for the sale of accounts and contract rights. List of Century 21 offices. Sparco Memo Book with list of old sets.

Central Drawer:

1 rubber band: green. Instructions on how to load Pez dispenser. $7.50 birthday gift certificate to company store. message pad. Referral thank you card from 1st Carolina Home Equity. Western Union highlighter. Western Union map of area codes and time zones. Employee suggestion form. Old postcard of Sex Pistols with little factoid "Who was Pauline?" 3 Washington Public Power District pens. Fountain Pentel Unibel pen. Numerous paper clips (okay: 39 big, 30 small). Canadian nickel. 5 Queen Elizabeth pennies. 32 Abe Lincoln pennies, 4 small, 1 heavy duty clips.

Top Right:

Spiderman Pez dispenser. Avon moisture therapy hand cream. Yellow post-its. Scotch tape and dispenser. 2 pairs — scissors. 1 staple puller. Stapler. Phillips screw driver. Sunglasses. Box of staples. Forms to order coupon books 1996 Western Union Directory. 2 bottles of whiteout. Box of forks/spoons/knives. Box of memo pads. Check-o-matic forms. Voucher requisitions. Credit card slips. Message pad. 1994 baseball cards (16 cards and a piece of Walter Spahn puzzle). 1997 & 1998 memo books.

Left Lower:

Suspense file. Trimsetter Times (Volume 4. 1999). Tatty old coverless Rand/McNally 1984 atlas. Collection of old files to reuse. The "Yellow Book" — Asset recovery collection guide.

Left Middle:

1999 Telecom USA Seattle phone book. Copy of 5-21-99 National Enquirer. "Feelin Ruff" sticker I got at last visit to Dr. Gold satin hot pants. Copy of Geraldo Rivera show "Zombies in Haiti." Blue Cross/Blue Shield insurance packet. Front page of Seattle Post-Intelligencer 7-15-98. Box of ultra-thin ribbed Trojans.

As Walter had just completed this crucial task of scrivener and inventory, panic all of the sudden broke out amongst the office ranks of Trimsetter Collections Dept. as a woman shrieked, "BJ's been shot!... BJ's been shot!... BJ's been shot!" in a mix of questions and exclamations of disbelief. All office activity ceased as the messenger was swarmed by the shocked and frightened. Walter puts down his pen and stands up in a noble gesture of concerned solidarity and listens to the garbled account delivered by the flipped-out secretary/aerobics instructor Miss Johnson, "BJ went to trailer to deliver the papers as the special forces were hot wiring the Cadillac... and," as tears streamed down the mistress's face about the loss of her lover, "and gunfire erupted from inside the trailer..."

"What!? Who!? Why!?" the people shouted out in unison.

"First at the special forces agents who were inside revving up the Cadillac... the Special Forces returned fire at the trailer as BJ was running back in terror to the company car, he got shot in a hail of bullets."

"BJ got shot?!... O no! What?! Who?! Why?!" went the chorus with so many ooohs and aaaahs like a Dr. Seus Christmas special.

"And they left him there to die as they sped off in the Cadillac and company car — they just left him! The police just called — he died on his way to the hospital... and..."

"DOA! Ohhhh Ahhhhh" as great cries of sorrow and wails of despair emanated throughout the room; the hysteria and grief became communal, more ooohs and aaaahs... what about his wife? does she know? has anyone gotten a hold of his wife!? Ooooh aaaaah... dead on arrival... shot... wife... she's pregnant, at the hospital... what hospital?... o no pregnant! I didn't know... BJ's wife... but I'm his lover! I am too! baby, baby... shot dead... shot from trailer... trailer trash! Shot by white trash! Trailer Trash! Trash! Trash! Baby! Shot dead! Kill! Kill! Kill! The cathartic frothing frenzy continued with all involved except for a slightly nonplussed Walter who was attempting to put a few more of the pieces of this puzzle together — his mind begins to work out a schemata of the events that led to this dramatic outcome. Just as he was connecting a few of the dots together, Crisis Manager Senior Vice President of Personnel Dale Martinet arrived to take control of the crisis situation and get the story made clear for everyone involved at Trimsetter Corporation and deliver a nice and tidy eulogy for BJ.

"Thank you Miss Johnson, that will be enough... hrumph, hrumph... Attention Trimsetter people... people... people... attention Trimsetter people... attention could I get everybody to calm down for just a minute... I'm sure by now you've all heard the tragic, tragic news that has befallen us — our dear friend and great performer shot dead in the line of duty for the greater glory of all us here at the family we like to call Trimsetter Corporation. BJ's concern was our firm's concern and our firm's concern was BJ's concern as well as our world view. As I'm sure most of you know, BJ and I were very close. BJ was like a son to me and as I'm sure most of you know I lost my only son in Vietnam, back in Khe Sahn; fightin off the Viet Cong!... and now I've lost BJ." Tears began to well up in Dale's eyes, but never a teardrop falls; like a crocodile, Walter thinks. Group sniffling continues as the maintenance crew forklifts in a pallet of Kleenex boxes.

"We've lost BJ. All of us!" as his voice booms, "But we here at Trimsetter Corporation never forget our boys! BJ was doing his job like my son was doing his job over in Vietnam! Fighting Communism, Fighting for Capitalism! for the Company! for his wife! his family! his country! and God! We here at Trimsetter Corporation support our troops!"

The maintenance crew began handing out MIA/POW flags and yellow ribbons. Dale pauses and as on Q a loud thunderous round of exuberant hand clapping occurred. He waves them down. Sets them at ease, smiling, thanking them. Distraction was his game.

"The story I've been told… was that BJ went to a certain domicile to address some discrepancies and in-corrections in an account and the bastards just shot him! Shot him down! Shot him down like a dog!" Dale's voice really booms on that and the effect is electric as corporate gasps of horror break out. "By the time 911 was called and the paramedics and police arrived BJ was choking out on his own blood — he died in the ambulance on his way to the hospital. That is all I've been told. That is all I know. That is what happened."

"What about the special forces repo men? the black helicopters? The repossession of the Cadillac!?" some of the people yammer.

Dale waves them all off as if they were all so many pesky nonsensical gnats and battering nabobs — chortling a bit, "Now, now rumors, rumors, rumors… people get excited, people get scared and start saying all kinds of crazy stuff about black helicopters and secret agents and a multitude of unknown knowns and known unknowns. Rest assured people, Trimsetter is great and powerful company with many jealous enemies who spread this kind of vicious, silly nonsense to wreak havoc and weaken us which is you. BJ was working like Marshall Dillon from Gun Smoke as a lone representative for the company to try and assist a client resolve a difference and a problem that had arisen with our company and… and sometimes misunderstandings and irrationality superimposes itself upon some human beings and… people die. It's just that simple people. So I'd like to get all this childish talk of black ops, black helicopters, Blackwater and repo-men and Cadillacs and Monte Carlos to cease!" Dale rallied with righteous indignation to admonish the children — his children. "So let's remember one thing, if the police happen to come around and start asking questions — funny questions — just remember: loose lips sink ships… it's got to stop… we're all in this together. So just remember, BJ was working alone to resolve a matter of difference upon Trimsetter's behalf and a client's. Could have been a marital/

domestic violence dispute as far as we know and BJ just got caught in the crossfire. According to what the police have informed me the assailant and murderer of BJ was apprehended, but died of wounds in police custody. Now I'd like us all to take a moment of silence in memory of BJ and after that a basket will be out front in which all Trimsetter employees can give a donation to a milk fund, I mean trust fund… to establish a trust fund for BJ's pregnant widow and family."

A half minute ticked by.

"Alright thank you for all your attention and time — it has been an awful morning for all of us here at Trimsetter Corporation. Now let's get back to work and make some money! Let's do it for BJ! For the company!" Dale walked out and then everybody went back to being like ruminants. Even Walter was shocked at the abrupt about face like it was already a fleeting memory as if they had all drunk from the water from the River Lethi — forget Greek mythology; call it the Hale-Bop Comet/Bhopal Effect Syndrome. TV Nation his mind said — with the attention span of a goldfish; and he was just beginning to feel like giving and receiving hugs. He returns to his desk to start reconnecting the dots now with Dr. Dale's gems of disinformation and misinformation that had been added to the tabooli. It was all becoming much clearer to him. BJ went off this morning like a good soldier with the special forces in an unmarked Buick, arriving upon the area of interest, they were of course much more acquainted with the risks involved, thus assigned BJ with his confident and superior gung-ho attitude to go up as a diversion to the hapless debtors eeking out their existence in the aluminum trailer who happened to have enough trouble reading especially when it came to the fine print parts that none of us ever read. Illiteracy is bliss. As BJ saunters up so merrily and begins rap-tap-tapping on the rickety door, the men from the black helicopters rappel down and work with the Chevrolet Caprice forces on the ground to repo the one asset of value — a fine Cadillac, well sort of fine. Well somebody obviously noticed and didn't like what they were seeing and let go with a volley of buckshot at the repo-men. Naturally, BJ's complexion changed as he took off with fear in his eyes from the trailer running.

Running, running, running — Running Man to meet a hail of .40 automatic hollow-point projectiles from the return fire of the special agents Glocks as they were just doing their job shooting back at the aloo-minimum trailer — a simple matter of self-defense. It's just too bad for BJ to happenchance get caught in the middle of it all. BJ — he be dead, and come to think about it as Walter recollected — BJ was a prick. Walter had no idea why all these people had been crying except for Chuck who was his racquetball partner and Miss Johnson, of course, who was going to miss the afternoon wee-wah sessions between aerobic Zumba workouts. 'Course the special forces dudes in the ninja outfits made escape with the Cadillac. Or Monte Carlo. Witnesses? What witnesses? If there were any left alive out of the melee — they'd be taken care of one way or another be it monetarily or otherwise… Like the JFK assassination … this world, what a world, where's Oliver Stone? — Trimsetter Corporation. Only one thing, how is Trimsetter and the police going to explain an aluminum trailer riddled with bullets and at least, two dead guys and a shotgun? Lawyers… good lawyers and money, lots of money. The coroner in the autopsy probably won't even find any birdshot on BJ's body, but instead find a cadaver littered with 9mms, .44 magnum rounds etc… from an assortment of Colts, Berettas, Glock 17s, and Rugers and God knows what else. Who knows — they say the special agents usually carry the Glock 23s, but those compact P-10 Para-Ordnance 11 shot .45 autos were becoming popular tiny packages for the black helicopter guys, at least, according to BJ, so it goes. They've probably already planted the necessary equipment to make it look like what they want it to be. BJ's got 5 or 6 guns on him, the poor sot in the trailer has got an arsenal to shame an Idaho militia. All very sinister Walter thinks; what is this, death on the installment program? Walter has the strange feeling he is being watched. Closely observed, in fact, maybe they were even reading his mind. It could be the paranoia from the drugs. He wish he could wrap his head in aluminum foil — at least keep the animals from reading his mind. Walter didn't advocate drug use in any way, shape or form — except like — If You Got ANY! No, he just preferred them mucho even though he knew it was just the way the Man was keeping him down. For being 99% chimp he didn't think he was doing too bad.

Just then Walter, contemplating the casual relationship with truth, noticed Michelle, a pretty receptionist who won the coveted friendly and most enthusiastic employee of the month award last August, was passing out mems around the office. She gave one to Walter.

It read:

Attention all employees. Due to the tragic incident that occurred today, detectives from the police may come around to ask some of you a few questions. Mister Ziggy Jaeger, Founder and Owner and We, the Management, request that you be most cooperative with the police and tell them nothing. Grief counselors will be arriving tomorrow at 10:00 am to assist in the recovery process.

Thank You — the Management

Later on that day, with creeping passivity, Walter, feeling content in his part of being part of the low information crowd; punched out at the same time, same place, wondering if it was a Cadillac or a Monte Carlo? The next morning, when he arrived at his cubicle/feeding station he immediately noticed that BJ's desk had been completely cleared out and remnants of files, records, pencils, and family photos. No vestiges of BJ's existence in that office were left, other than in the hallway where he's in the group photo of the company picnic/white-water rafting jamboree hung. BJ front row, second to the left, sharp teeth. Maybe they're commissioning a bronze statue of him? Walter felt compelled to immediately check his file cabinet rifling thru them till he came to the left middle drawer where he had left a copy of yesterday's work of his desk inventory. It was all gone. A sinking feeling overcame Walter, he was being watched.

Meanwhile, Hank was working on another one of his memoirs; the erudite German professor, the intellectual adventurer, the Cold War hero and possibly the reincarnation of Metternich. He had saved the country countless times now, but he couldn't save Nixon. He had brought peace to the Mid-East, Indochina, Cyprus, Chile, checked and contained the specter of communism, opened up the Chi-Coms doors to business, brokered the Paris Peace Accords to bring the American boys home, the POWs, save face for America from defeat — moral defeat. It was not military defeat. We were bombing them into the Stone Age — O wait, much of the culture of Laos, Cambodia and Vietnam was already in the stone age. Nonetheless! — the military had just got tired of all the killing. A little power going to the id, perhaps? Now we've gotten smarter and call it "collateral damage." Damnit! First it was the boots on the ground and eventually the mutiny like a cancer got to the air force and navy. Sir! No Sir! What could we do but withdraw the troops and erase the divisive and unpleasant word "Vietnam" from the newspapers. No more evening KIA and body count reports from Walter Cronkite. Yes, Henry's regime had done many wonderful things. He'd even won the Nobel Peace Prize — one must suppose, all part of "Stockholm Syndrome" — poor peace. If it wasn't for that little chain-smoking Italian bitch Fallaci… o Nixon, sick in his nerves, chewed me out for that one. Called me names. Mocked me for talking about being a cowboy. Here I go, as a child, escape from the clutches of Nazi Germany like Madame Secretary (of State) we have today — Madeleine Albright — (with thick German accent) embrace this country, save this country and what kind of thanks do I get. How about the Kissinger Doctrine of establishing "stable regimes" in Latin America? Let us not forget East Timor? It was all done to maintain this CIA/Pentagon archipelago in order that Southeast Asia remain in the Free World. What did Bismarck say: There is a Providence that protects idiots, drunkards, children and the United States of America. That WTO thing's gonna be a mess. Why is there always pandemonium? I think I'll go to Geneva instead; get out the loofa, get a massage, have a cocktail, look out over the Lake.

Chapter Six

Che

Whatever begins to be tranquil is gobbled up by something that is not tranquil.

William Randolf Hearst

As Walter and Mac come in from the wet after another sortie upon the rainy streets of Seattle, they are greeted by Maurice in a wife-beater and a Gaulois cigarette hanging from the side of his mouth. Mac shakes off the umbrella. Maurice grunts and says to Mac, "Marines do not carry umbrellas…" Walter for the first time saw Mac caught off guard, saw that that remark stung a bit, kind of caught Mac right in the jimmys. Mac just narrowed his eyes at Maurice. Walter was surprised at how fit and buff Maurice was — he had only seen him wearing nice loose silk dress shirts. (Except on those occasions in the morning when Maurice pranced around in his French thong, but Walter would always turn and look the other way — it was a speedo thing…) The big meeting was about to begin — of desire armed.

Mac commences the meeting at the gallery assemblage of ELF/ ALF, Sandinistas and feministas, anarchists from Eugene and a platoon of insane clown posse with: "A Molotov cocktail is a bottle containing three parts kerosene and one part motor oil. The bottle is sealed and wrapped in waste cotton, which is sprinkled with gasoline and ignited. When hurled against a target the bottle breaks and burning kerosene spreads a sheet of flame."

The assemblage is a loose group of cells not exactly into "peaceful liberal protest" at the upcoming WTO powwow. Gandhi is MIA; could even be a POW. Get out the POW/MIA flag… probably thousands of them still stuck in North Korea! Manchuria! North Viet-Nam! and the Government knows all about it and isn't doing a damn thing about it! Anyway — we digress… again, better call Sean Hannity.

Mac goes on in free association, all part of the American Warrior Free Fighting System — "By night a direct attack is always preferable. Creativity plus a machine gun is an unstoppable combination. It is possible to capture an encampment if there is enough drive and necessary presence of mind and if the risks are not excessive.

An encirclement requires waiting and taking cover, closing in steadily on the enemy, trying to harass him in every way, and above all, trying to force him by fire to come out. When the circle has been closed to short range, the "Molotov cocktail" is a weapon of extraordinary effectiveness. Before arriving at a range for the "cocktail" shotguns with a special charge can be employed. These arms, christened in our war with the name "M-16," consist of a 16-calibre sawed-off shotgun with a pair of legs added in such a way with a butt of the gun they form a tripod. The weapon will thus be mounted at an angle of about 45 degrees; this can be varied by moving the legs back and forth. It is loaded with an open shell from which all the shot has been removed. A cylindrical stick extending from the muzzle of the gun is used as the projectile. A bottle of gasoline resting on a rubber base is placed on the end of the stick. This apparatus will fire the burning bottles a hundred meters or more with a fairly high degree of accuracy. This is an ideal weapon for encirclements when the enemy has many wooden or inflammable material constructions; also for firing against tanks in hilly country. Best to lay a direct, steady enfilade…

Once the encirclement ends with a victory, or, having completed its objectives, all platoons retire in order to the place where the backpacks have been left, and normal life is resumed. The nomadic life of a guerilla fighter in this stage produces a deep sense of fraternity.

Sabotage is one of the invaluable arms of a people that fights... Keep things imbalanced with — misdirection, stealth tactics, throw your shoes, whatever it takes. I think if you're not ready to fight the police, you shan't let them pick you up and carry you off. You must recognize that you are not ready to fight to the very ends of your principles. Dissidence is Here! The Triumph of Will! Let us not do this protesting for nice liberal white people! Get-up! Stand-up!... Stand-up for your rights!

You are the Vanguard! Re-education Camps! Indoctrination should be continuous! You are the Intelligentsia! As Mao Tse Tung says! Change must come... through the barrel... of a gun!

All this is achieved by wide-scale organization of the masses supplemented with patient and careful education of the facts of the Revolution. Vigilance against any bourgeois manifestations opposed to the Revolution should also be constant; and vigilance over morale within the revolutionary masses should be stricter. Collective work for collective ends, ought to be cultivated. Workers and Peasants will approach the fulfillment of the plan with watershed determination and wholehearted selflessness, and at all cost despite all hardship! Volunteer brigades to construct roads, bridges, docks, dams and schools should receive a strong impulse; these serve to forge a unity among persons showing their love for the Revolution with works. Fascism! Fight the Power! With the sweat of his brow men shall eat bread! It's a free concert man... and the Re-vo-lu-Shin... will be televised! Go forward! O yea Lions of the Caliphate! And thus, there will be Peace in the Valley!"

Great applause from the Luddite masses — as Mac shouts above the din; Walter is amazed by the fervor as well as Mac's ability as provocateur in this festival of the oppressed. The Beastie Boys "Sabotage" gets playin way up loud. Amidst the billows of blue tobacco haze, Maurice stands silently in the shadows. Maurice comes up behind Walter and says, "Despair and misery are static factors. The dynamism of an uprising flows from hope and pride. Not actual suffering but the hope of better things incites people to revolt."

A man is found skulking near the gallery and is brought to Mac, the general-in-chief. At first, the man denies all knowledge of the enemy/police but a rope thrown around his neck and cast over the steel yardarm hook and pulley engine lift, brought him the use of his memory, and he gave an accurate and detailed account of his work as an informant, what the SPD and the FBI and the ATF and the NSA were up to etc... ammunition, supplies, armored personnel carriers, surveillance systems, numbers/amounts, and not forgetting two pretty little pieces of artillery commanding some of the streets; ready with grapeshot, for the barricades and enra`ge, Napoleon waits: the Situationist years, again. Unfortunately for himself, he let out the fact that he had been sent to gather news on the Manifesto Party and Ruckus, and hence was punished as a spy. But his information was so full and after severe cross-examination there was so little contradiction in his story, that Mac formed his plan of attack on the facts thus obtained. The result showed that the statements of the spy were entirely accurate. The fear of death had so discomposed his mind that he could not invent a lie. Call it enhanced interrogation. Walter quite upset and quite drunk, shouted at Mac, "You're going to get us all killed!"

Deadpan, Mac replies, "Then we'll all be together... But what about my thirst? — xin loi... xin loi."

And Baby Nambu adds, "a weeping sky... gives life to flowers. Rain on the leaves, soldiers sing. You never hear — anything... Drums of War. Xin loi... Clash muthafukker."

Mac adds, "And Walter, remember, the sorrowful mystery — Jesus was not punished, scourged and tortured by the wicked, bad men, but by the silence of good men. Some men will steal from their mother for the ends... you must be blessed. Read the tarot and know that fortune-telling is for lunatics and old ladies. Buck the saw, man. It's time for the countdown. The I'Ching: Sung K'an —

Conflict. Follow your muse. This is your Paradise... Crystal clear, clear as ice..."

Walter leaves the others with his mind bended without the benefits of chemical augmentation and returns to his spare dank subversive quarters to do some reading that Maurice had recommended and to forget about the imbroglio he has found himself in... as well as the rumors of war. Problem, problem, problem... his brain tells him; insane as it ever was... insane as it ever was. He hopes the spy is ok.

He reads: "The most loathsome materialism is not the kind people usually think of, but the sort that attempt to let dead ideas pass for living realities, diverting sterile myths." — Camus. Walter pauses and reflects, he reads on: "The greatest defeat, in anything, is to forget, and above all to forget what it is that has smashed you, and to let yourself be smashed without ever realizing how thoroughly devilish men can be. When our time is up, we people must not bear malice, but neither must forget: we must tell the whole thing, without altering one word — everything that we have seen of man's viciousness and then it will be over and time to go. That is enough of a job for a whole lifetime." — Celine. Thus Walter fell asleep, in his palatial digs, dreaming of orchids.

Part 2

Chapter Seven
All the Young Dudes

Where do bad people go when they die? They don't go to
heaven where the angels fly. They go to a lake of fire and
fry. Won't see'em again till the Fourth of Ju-ly!

"Lake of Fire" Kurt Cobain/Nirvana (Meat Puppets)

The forces of evil, the forces of good and the forces of
confusion were colliding together in a swirl upon the streets of Seattle
in a bozo nightmare... for the vanity fair of the WTO was in town
with a varied assortment of leaders, fools and imposters: just when
the city was starting to get cute. Foreigners in Wonderland — OZ.
The Seattle Police Department jogged in military cadence in full-riot
gear regalia as Storm-troopers or was it teenage-mutant ninja turtles,
while a few blocks away, folks wearing cute sea-turtle costumes in
protest to save the sea-turtles meandered peacefully in the streets
amongst other people there to save butterflies amongst others there
to just break things. It is a festive, hopeful Mardi-Gras like atmosphere like there really could be Peace in the Valley, if one could ignore the omnipresent, heavy-handedness of the SPD Storm-troopers
and armored personnel carriers — waitin to get that stranglehold
baby... The house of pain is in effect, yo! Keeping Fear Alive might
have made a nice banner. Mac, Maurice and Walter move about

downtown Seattle the day before the official opening of the WTO. For several weeks prior, Walter, Maurice, and Mac had, at least, it seemed to Walter, been doing a great deal of reconnaissance of the multitude of buildings and streets throughout the city. They moved on, it was a clear day, blue sky, cloudless, no wind. The late afternoon autumn sun was beginning to ebb and as they walked the shadows were long and the leaves falling loud. Walter liked the change of schedule. (Trimsetter had dismissed Walter for irregular activities. He now had a part-time job as a dishwasher at 13 Coins Restaurant — he likes working with his hands; yanking the trays off a conveyor belt and feeding their contents into an enormous foul-mouthed machine that roared and spat until its dishes and trays, free of the congealed fat, muck and gravy came steaming out the other end, fogging his glasses and filling the air with the harsh smell of chlorine — the heat and the noise; the yelling, shouting, stress, sweating and the fast pace Walter found exhilarating, almost liberating from the confines of Trimsetter Corp. Working with former convicts whose jobs were arranged through parole officers and work release programs, Walter would hang out in the back area by the dumpsters, passing out a lot of free cigarettes, hoping in listening to these felons that something profound might reveal itself… from a lifetime of regret having spent the better part of their lives behind bars. But no, they just mostly wanted to get out of doing their jobs, score free ciggies from Walter and take their extended smoke breaks, throw dice, play cards and sometimes even sneaking off to the stockrooms and having sex. So much for lessons garnered from a lifetime of regret. Bad, bad luck). Making trenchant observations, calling in points and coordinates, having Walter take notes, looking about through binoculars, Mac and Maurice went about their esoteric business. It wasn't French, but they spoke in a language Walter could only half understand — a military lingua franca. He heard something about, "This will make a good LZ if we need to bring in Delta or a SEAL team… could lay some benign terror with a little C-4; maybe we should — mine the harbor, like Haiphong. Or Nicaragua." Elliot Bay looked so peaceful with the Ferris wheel slowly turning, the plumes of the white sails and the ships silently gliding by… Walter cringed, they must be joking. Then Mac turns to Walter and sez: "Grab hold of your junk and get your man-pants on Walter, Mickey Mouse is in da house, it's going to be a bumpy ride. Stop-time baby, like an affliction — the 9th configuration. Jump into the fire... we just gonna pour some gasoline..." It was all very covert — undercover. That's how Walter felt, with his scraggly beard and his disheveled look and his Black Flag t-shirt on (people were shying away from him on the street; kind of empowering) — he was working undercover, pulling into various haunts and dives with the general banter with many of the usual suspects, but now they were encountering suits, as well, like businessmen, but hard ones, not particularly jovial, profitable ones. Sprechen zee deutsch baby... Walter thought he heard German being spoken. The envoys were lean, rugged-looking with weathered faces, hard eyes and erect carriages. Walter was introduced and one "German" shook hands with Walter and regarded him with an appraising, unwavering stare. Walter's eager smile was returned with a bleak one from this German. Boches! Walter also believes he might have seen Señor Agape dressed up like a penguin — in protest, of course. Back already from Benares, the City of the Dead... Walter was trying to figure out the calculus in this tournament of shadows — he thought, shit we're still trying to figure out who killed Kennedy and did Courtney have Kurt shot? So as Doctor Hunter proclaimed: When it gets weird, the weird turn pro... Next thing you know, Andre will pop up. Walter was beginning to have that surrounded, encroaching, asphyxiating, can't breathe feeling like, back in high school, when his parents, lit on wine, for his "own good" sent him, in a pre-emptive strike to gay camp, cuz they thought he might be gay — hair long, smokes dope. He just wasn't athletic like Gunnar, his alpha male father, nor interested in them. Not good in sports; must be gay! Gunnar's goddam queer steer son... O the shame, the shame — Oh well, he was thinking maybe under the pretext of the WTO protests, it would give him an existentialist, surrealist excuse to get with Danger Woman — somehow. She's so beautiful — paints her eyes black as night and wears a cross around her neck, o the pain, the pain, cuts like a knife; just hurts to see... to feel, it's so deep. Vicious... Last lipstick postcard dispatches from Andre were from the Horn of Africa: Somalia and Yemen (gettin near Abu Dhabi Dum and the Kingdom of the Holy Land) "I'm sure it's some sort of great humanitarian intervention he is on." Walter thought. An obtuse message in a bottle is sent — with poems — the messages have a political context: "I'm waiting for my stimulus payment from the government for which I'm selling my silence and agreeing to the efficacy of our Very Noble War on Terror —

5 Long Bloody in Iraq

Wanted for Victory:

Conformity, Blind Allegiance, Complacency, Uniformity, Silence, Renounce Your Liberties

OR THE TERRORISTS WIN!

Mogadishu:

Walter, I sit here smoking a cigarette at 3:30 am with a vo- tive candle and a full moon lit night — wind, sand and stars... O Saint Jude, patron saint of hopeless cases and lost causes; some velvet morning, when I'm straight — I pray to thee... Oscar Wilde is in the room with me... the poisonous smoke wafts up from the ash tray, a steady curlish blue stream, I try to decipher its meaning... of what was everything... What tempest brews ye? There ain't no asylum here... King Soloman don't live around here... go straight to hell, boy... go straight to hell, as I stare at an infinity of abstrac- tions — Muslim Art, it's all right there? The Clash. It's like French kissing the bully... Viva Zapata! Viva Sandinista! Viva Zapatistas, Chiapas! Viva Mia Zapata! And remember Walter, you've got to be cheerful with women — in the beginning, at least. First poem: Dan- ger Woman — in excelsior   the sardonic laugh   She   the gray wolf eyes   with sharp black dots   pupils   gypsy eyes!   looking at one's   looking thru one's   piercing   reading   like the cards of the tarot   one's soul...   on ice   shivers   and then she smiles wispy...   the wind   smoke   truth   the second poem reads: (from Danger Woman) En Garde   "I who are you to move me as if I were a chess piece   shove me into the stiff pattern of a knight

frustrate me with position of a pawn   why can't I be Queen?   is
that beyond the conventions   of the game   that I might move
where   I please" (Walter hears a cello plays somewhere) Christmas
in Belfast: That's when I got this from her. It fukked me up, I wrote
her — "Came reeling out of the tavern that night, in pain, agony,
missing you — found myself at Midnight Mass; very drunk. Don't
know what happened... woke up, Dawn, in a confessional. You have
driven me to God and drink."

Walter, the deal was done in Denmark on a dark and stormy
night; an opportunity arose and I was just an innocent bystander...
movin a few diamonds here in Ireland. Walter gasps and shouts
aloud, "Yeah Andre! Blood diamonds from the Congo! Leopold's
ghost hovers. Just a little "Let's Go!" to northern Ireland — just pass
them on to the IRA for a few more bombs! Perfect Andre, hope
you don't forget your Eurail pass! The incorrigible, entitled dandy! O
the lonely planet... poor old Buddha... Then Walter thinks: What
would Rocky Bleier do? — he'd fight back! O well, O my, Walter
thinks, knowing that the raven-haired Danger Woman was raped
by her step-father to the song "Whiskey River" — she could dance
that song real good — swinging around the stripper pole. Walter
picked her up a couple of times at the shady little non-descript building with the sign Talents West on Lake City Way. It had a small
placard in front of the parking stalls that read: Italians Only. Vaffanculo! (Italian Yiddish for — go fuk yourself) Walter thinks. Rick's
Club, which took it's name from the movie Casablanca (no shit, an
ex-doorman/bouncer he worked with in a cannery up in Yakutat
told Walter that one) where she mostly worked was just down the
road. She rounded out her career as a sort of den mother at one
of the stripper houses provided by the familia. Walter remembers
as tears came to her eyes when she heard that the old padrone had
finally died — peacefully in his sleep — she hadn't heard the news;
he presumed she already knew. He thought, what a world. Walter
was feeling like really getting some red, red wine, keep him rockin all
of the time, make him feel so fine... all of the time. Gimme shelter.
This is a love story, Walter sez to himself and then he thinks — O
Lord won't you just buy me, a Mercedes Benz... as the ballad on the

streets takes a heavy portent as he notices Mac flashing signals with a mirror to Baby Nambu who is up top the Camlin Hotel across from the Washington State Convention Center as he signals back to Mac and Maurice, the operator/provocateurs. Like Apache Indians. Walter thinks, maybe I should check myself into an institution for inebriates. Then he thinks: maybe we need a bigger boat. Jets fly high as contrails disperse, spreading cob-web like filaments milky-white, into cloud cover.

Andre gets to Marseilles via some hashish deal out of Kurdistan and checks the Poste Restante and finds a letter addressed to him from the maven Adrian Bissette aka Danger Woman. It was dated from August 27. It reads: "I was at the beach yesterday. The beach makes me crazy. The sand on my feet was so sensory. There was fine dry sand that slipped through my toes and wet sand that gave a little when I stepped on it, but was so warm and inviting to my feet. There was the slightest warm breeze and the sun hitting my bare skin was the perfect temperature. Not too hot, but warming my core. The best part was I saw a private shady place in the distance. On the sand and under the trees. Tucked away. I wanted you to lie me down on that cozy beach and then lie next to me under a light summer throw. And then peel off my clothes while you are kissing me gently. And then rub your hands all over my skin. And then pull me close to you and slowly and sweetly fuck me for, maybe a few hours. Until I bite my lip. Until I scrunch up my face with pain and pleasure. Until I let my excited screams slip accidently from my lips. Until I can see the prints from you hands on my skin. Until my breasts are sore. Until all my sexual energy has filled us both up. Until I'm suffering from hunger and thirst. Until I simply can't take anymore…" Andre caught the first flight out to Seattle, leaving on a jet airplane. The heart is a lonely hunter. Can't find a better man…

Beck's "Loser" plays steady in the background: Louis Willy went tracking thru the downtown streets amazed at some of the circus beginning to develop just before the crucible of the WTO kickoff. He didn't know about no WTO and thought NAFTA if you HAFTA. But he damn sure knew the communists were behind the anti-war movement! They're against War, the military, guns and huntin! They're against even lettin a dog have a pair of balls! Wait till the Rapture hits, that'll show'em. It'd be nice to get some accuracy in media rather than all this infotainment and politically-correct revisionism of historee! He thought this was just regular old Seattle Left Coast Fifth Column Za-Za-Land. He is perplexed with his encounter with Adolf Mungu and wondering where exactly his nemesis Walter Curmudgeon could be. He recollected back to his army days along the DMZ in Korea. It felt more normal back there than here. This would make a varmint shooter's dream. He was a country boy at heart — he didn't need all these fuckin city problems. Scanning the street theatre with all the happy campers and men on stilts and unicycles and jugglers with funny hats and weird beards wearing kilts, and painted ladies and satyrs and people dressed like fuzzy critters. Bring you up, bring you down — more tales of ordinary madness. Louis Willy cinched up his belt, carrying his bindle stick, preparing for Y2K and the Zombie Apocalypse. Soon the bats in the belfry would be flying. We need to destroy the village in order to save it. The Apex Predator lurks onward. Thunder rumbles in the distant mountains… far from the maddening crowd. Airplanes circle moaning overhead.

Chapter Eight

Control

> The need for constantly expanding markets for its products chases the bourgeoisie over the entire surface of the globe. It must nestle everywhere, settle everywhere, establish connections everywhere.
>
> *The Communist Manifesto – Karl Marx/Friedrich Engels*

What is the WTO? The World Trade Organization (WTO) is the only global international organization dealing with the rules of trade between nations. At its heart are the WTO agreements, negotiated and signed by the bulk of the world's trading nations and ratified in their parliaments. The goal is to help producers of goods and services, exporters and importers conduct their business. The WTO is an organization that intends to supervise and liberalize international trade.

Back at the We B Art Gallery/Manifesto Party HQ: Señor Agape burst upon Walter in a penguin outfit — it was him! Mac took one look at Señor Agape and says, "The man's in un-good health. Appears a bit on the lavender side." He has been partying to excess in a Dionysian orgy with some of the sea turtles and he thought it was imperative that him and Walter — "attend a rosary and make prayer to St. Francis. Right away! — for the tonsure does not always destroy the earthly passions of the mortal. Time for the countdown! Here in Kicksville with the birds and the bees all gathering… It's all going to be tranquilo!" He tells Walter. "Tranquilo… And know, the end starts at the very beginning." He knows Walter is an atheist and Lutheran, but pas` problem. They jump on a 43 bus that's full of babooshkas, dervishes and Rosicrucians. Walter felt like Dorothy; like off to see the Wizard — heading to the U-District, towards Blessed Sacrament, a Dominican Parish.

It's a musty old church, Gothic and Romanesque — full of statues, stained glass and candles. They dip their hands in the marble fount of holy water and give the sign of the cross as people sang dirges in the dark. The full moon is in Pisces. It is just beginning: "In the name of the Father, and the Son and of the Holy Ghost. Amen. Hail Mary, full of grace, the Lord is with thee. Blessed art thou amongst women and blessed is the fruit of thy womb, Jesus. Glory to the Father, and the Son, and to the Holy Spirit. As it was in the beginning, is now, and will be forever. Amen. The Fatima prayer — O my Jesus, forgive us our sins, save us from the fire of hell, lead all souls to heaven especially those in most need of your mercy. Hail, holy Queen, Mother of mercy, our life, our sweetness and our hope. To thee do we cry, poor banished children of Eve: to thee do we send up our sighs, mourning and weeping in this valley of tears. Turn then, most gracious Advocate, thine eyes of mercy toward us, and after this our exile, show unto the blessed fruit of thy womb, Jesus, O Clement, O Loving, O sweet Virgin Mary! (Leader) Pray fur us, O Holy Mother of God. (All) That we may be made worthy of the promises of Christ. (Leader) Let us pray. (All) O God, Whose Only-Begotten Son, by His life, death and resurrection, has purchased for us the reward of eternal life: grant, we beseech Thee, that by meditating upon these mysteries in the most holy Rosary of the Blessed Virgin Mary, we may contain, and obtain what they promise, through the same Christ our Lord. Amen.

St. Michael the Archangel, Defend us in battle. Be our protection against the wickedness and snares of the Devil. May God rebuke him, we humbly pray, and do thou, O prince of the heavenly hosts, by the power of God, thrust into hell, Satan, and all evil spirits, who prowl about the world seeking the ruin of souls. Amen.

Litany to Jesus in the womb of Mary (Response to each of the invocations is: Have mercy on us) Jesus, conceived by the Holy Spirit in the womb of Mary. Have mercy on us. Jesus, uniquely human from the moment of conception in the womb of Mary. Have mercy on us. Jesus, present at creation, created in the womb of Mary. Have mercy on us. Jesus, through whom the world was made, formed in the womb of Mary. Have mercy on us. Jesus, word made flesh, taking on a human body in the womb of Mary. Have mercy on us. Jesus, revealed by the Father, concealed in the womb of Mary. Have mercy on us. Jesus, subject to human development in the womb of Mary. Have mercy on us. Jesus, whose Precious Blood first flowed through tiny arteries and veins in the womb of Mary. Have mercy on us. Jesus, hidden nine months in the womb of Mary. Have mercy on us. Jesus, only begotten of the Father, assuming flesh in the womb of Mary. Have mercy on us. Jesus, begotten by God, nourished by the substance and blood of his most Holy Mother in the womb of Mary. Have mercy on us. Jesus, leaping from eternity into time, in the womb of Mary. Have mercy on us. Jesus, revealing with His Father and the Holy Spirit all wisdom and knowledge to His Most Holy Mother, in the womb of Mary. Have mercy on us. Jesus, aware of His role as Redeemer in the womb of Mary. Have mercy on us. Jesus, Sanctifier of His Precursor from the womb of Mary. Have mercy on us. Jesus, Eternal Word, Divine Child, embraced by the Father, in the womb of Mary. Have mercy on us. Jesus, raising His Mother to the heights of sanctification, in the womb of Mary. Have mercy on us. Jesus, everlasting delight of heaven, in the womb of Mary. Have mercy on us. Jesus, manifesting His Incarnation to His Holy Mother, in the womb of Mary. Have mercy on us. Jesus, adored and contemplated by His Mother in the sanctuary of her womb. Have mercy on us. Jesus, before whom the angels prostrated themselves, in the womb of Mary. Have mercy on us. Jesus, in whom the very angels beheld the humanity of the Infant God and the union of the two natures of the Word in the virginal womb of Mary. Have mercy on us. Jesus, whose Holy Limbs first budded in the womb of Mary.

Have mercy on us. Jesus, whose Sacred Heart began beating in the womb of Mary. Have mercy on us. Jesus, whose Godhead the world cannot contain, weighing only a few grams in the womb of Mary. Have mercy on us. Jesus, Divine Immensity, once measuring only tenths of an inch in the womb of Mary. Have mercy on us. Jesus, whose Divine Grasp outreaches the universe, cradled in the womb of Mary. Have mercy on us. Jesus, Sacrificial Lamb, Docile Infant in the womb of Mary. Have mercy on us. Jesus, Who was to suffer the agony and passion of death, accepting the human capacity for pain and grief, in the womb of Mary. Have mercy on us. Jesus, foretelling His Eucharistic Presence, in the womb of Mary. Have mercy on us. Jesus, Lamb of God in the womb of Mary, spare us O Lord. Jesus, Holy Innocent in the womb of Mary, graciously hear us O Lord, have mercy on us. Jesus, Son of God and Messiah in the womb of Mary. Have mercy on us, O Lord. The Apostles Creed: I believe in God, the Father Almighty, And in Jesus Christ His only Son, Our Lord Who was conceived of the Holy Spirit Born of the Virgin Mary Suffered under Pontius Pilate was crucified, died and was buried. On the third day, he rose again He ascended into Heaven and is seated at the right hand of God, the Father Almighty. He will come again to judge the living and the dead. I believe in the Holy Spirit, the Holy Catholic Church, the Communion of Saints, the forgiveness of sins, the resurrection of the body, and life everlasting. Amen. Our Father: Our Father, who art in Heaven, hallowed be Thy name, Thy kingdom come, Thy will be done on earth as it is in Heaven. Give us this day our daily bread, and forgive us our trespasses as we forgive those who trespass against us. And lead us into temptation but deliver us from evil. Amen. Glory Be: Glory be to the Father and to the Son and to the Holy Spirit. As it was in the beginning is now, and ever shall be, world without end. Amen. To the Blessed Virgin Mary at Fatima: O my Jesus, forgive us our sins, save us from the fires of hell, lead all souls to Heaven, especially those who have most need of your mercy. Hail Mary: Hail Mary, full of grace, the Lord is with Thee. Blessed art Thou among women. And Blessed is the fruit of Thy womb, Jesus. Hail Mary, Mother of God Pray for us sinners now and at the hour of our death. Amen." And 150 Hail Marys' later and repetition of much of the other prayers of the Joyful Mysteries and the Luminous Mysteries and the Sorrowful Mysteries and the Glorious Mysteries; they finished. And with the votive candles flickering like fireflies dancing about them; Walter realized that humor was our way of dealing with fear and anxiety and that there is no humor without death. What a vendetta.

Señor Agape and Walter walk a few blocks to polish off the evening drinking tequila at a joint with an appropriate name and ambiance called Dante's. Señor Agape, as they sit there, still further warming their souls with a few shots of Hornitos, ses to Walter, "You know Walter — the emblematic crown of thorns may be worn by those possessed little of the spirit of humility which adorned the Holy Redeemer." With that Walter ordered another round thinking that might aid him in his moment of doubt of Señor Agape's general sanity. He heads to the men's room admiring some of the devilish decor of the public house and coming upon some script on the wall he reads: Thus from the boughs, an unknown voice called down. And thus warned, Virgil, Statins, and myself drew close, and hugged the cliff, and hurried on. "Recall," the voice went on, "those cursed beasts born of a cloud. When they had swilled the wine, Theseus had to slash their double breasts. Recall those Jews who once showed Gideon how to abandon all to thirst, where at he would not lead them down the hills to Mideon." So we strode on along the inner way while the voice cried the sins of Gluttony which earn, as we had seen, such fearful pay — The Divine Comedy: Purgatorio. Walter pulls his pud, shakes no more than three times and returns to find Señor Agape rapturously engaged in talking with some Moroccans — Berbers. Señor Agape gets talking of the Atlas Mountains and hash oil and Marrakesh and Gene Genet and Sharia Law and Franco and the Spanish Foreign Legion and the Alhambra and Andalusia and Moorish Spain. Then Señor Agape qualifies that, "Drinking is part of our religion." And he begins to recite: "Knight I am and knight I will die, if it pleases Almighty God. Some choose the broad road of proud ambition; some that of mean and servile flattery; some that of deceitful hypocrisy, and a small number that of true religion; but I influenced by my star, follow the narrow path of knight errantry, and in practicing that calling I despise wealth but not honour. I have redeemed injuries, righted wrongs, chastised insolence, conquered giants and trampled on monsters. I am in love, for no other reason than it is an obligation for knight-errant to be so; but though I am, I am no lustful lover, but one of the chaste, platonic kind. My intentions are always directed towards virtuous ends, to do good to all and evil to none. O where art thou Dulcinea?" And he looks at the Berbers piercingly with flashing tequila eyes as he wags his talisman — "U call it corn, we call it maiz. U call it Allah or Yahweh, we call it the Trinity with God, Jesus and the Holy Ghost and some people say that corn and maiz don't exist! As we seek our blue print to the after-life! Allez Walter! Allez Walter! We need to catch the bus! And with that, our fine Muslim brothers, we bid you adieu." Thus spoke Zarathustra, thus they caught the buzzy bus back to a warehouse on East Denny — another meeting place; part factory, part barracks, the mosh pit of the direct action plans. Large puppets and a siege tower were being constructed there, all to prepare for the coming day. And as the Bermuda Triangle closes and the Trojan Horse comes together… somewhere out there, on stereo, way up loud, across the Seattle city nightscape; James Brown is wailing — "This is a man's world!"

Chapter Nine
N30 — An Epic Day

There will be no more Hope. No more Glory. Not for the nation. Not for the world, I daresay. There will be no more parades.

Ford Maddox Ford

As the tempest brews, several thousand had gathered that Monday at the United Methodist Church which was the headquarters of the grassroots NGOs. They were to march to the convention center. It was the environment day and the Earth Island Institute had put together the sea turtle costumes for the marchers to wear. The sea turtles became the prime symbol of the WTO's threat to the environmental laws when a WTO tribunal ruled that the U.S. Endangered Species Act, which requires shrimp to be caught with turtle extruder devices, was an unfair trade barrier. Now the question is — what is eco-terrorism?

Along with the environmental marchers on the street that Monday morning, was a showing of labor union members from the Steelworkers and the Longshoremen. A Polish solidarity — enough to make St Francis and Lech Walensa weep with joy as a large banner read "Teamsters and Turtles Together at Last!" But alas, not all is well, all this marching was already interfering with the Christmas shoppers, some of whom were getting angry enough to begin their own spree of a Black Friday/Walmart combi of rioting while shopping by clubbing some of the turtle protesters like baby seals. But there were to be no arrests of the mad shoppers this week.

So the nice courteous police-escorted march makes its way to the protest pen at the convention center. The head of the Sierra Club gives a speech; Friends of the Earth give a speech. And others. All in varying degrees critical or not critical of Clinton/Gore and NAFTA (if you HAFTA). The WTO is excoriated, genetically-engineered food is vilified as Frankenstein food and something referred to as "free trade" is critiqued. After all the speechifying, Jose Bove, a sheep farmer from southern France and probably a Cathar leads a contingent to a McDonald's to hand out rounds of Roquefort cheese in protest to the U.S. decision to impose a heavy tariff on Roquefort cheese in retaliation for the European Union's refusal to import American hormone-treated beef. It's all in the details.

Bove, a chief of the Confederation Paysanne, a French environmental group is already awaiting trial for destroying a cache of Novarti's genetically-engineered corn in Larzac, France where a McDonald's was being constructed. Bove is militant in halting this worldwide mad logic and demands, not clemency but justice! Bove gives a rousing speech against the evils of Monsanto and bovine growth hormone and Roundup Ready soybeans. Basically, according to the science, some of this stuff is messing with the building block of biology — pollen: which affects the birds, bees and butterflies. Monarch butterflies, for instance, are taking a helluva hit. Kind of like — no honey, no life. Breaking it down, you know, it's all in the details.

Thus ensued, after the rousing speech by Bove, the crowd storms the McDonald's, breaking a few windows and urging the customers and workers to join the marchers on the streets. The cops who had been marching and parading around in militaristic cadence in the downtown vicinity, showed up moments later in their black Darth Vader attire and black armored personnel carriers — On the nightly news, the TV anchors affectionately referred to them as "the Peacekeepers" — Thus the first glass was broken in what Cockburn and St. Clair would later dub "the five days that shook the world" in the Battle of Seattle. But the cops refrained from violence and just opted to display their potential firepower. They cordoned off a four block area until the crowd dribbled away an hour or so later. Soon things would change; you could feel it, feel it…

Reveille: Walter wakes up very early that morning before the official beginning day of the WTO to the blaring sound of "Peace Train" by Yusef Of The No-Fly List, better known as Cat Stevens. Mac was playing it way up loud, he explained, "— kind of psyche everybody up — u'know."

"It's 4 o'clock in the morning!"

"I know we've got to get ready. Time is tight… time is tight… Get down to Victor Steinbrueck Park."

The Setting: the Clampdown is nearing. N30 has broken. It is going to be an epic day. On a marquee at the Lusty Lady it reads: Welcome Nude World Order! The cops on the street knew Seattle was in for a real shit-storm even with all the intense WMD and SWAT riot control training and exercises. They even got instruction from the Secret Service dignitary protection and escort service (there were rumors that half the call girls in Vegas had come to town). Might have to check out that escort service thing. Vice Squad! Also, they attended seminars on protest methods, tactics and strategies hosted by the FBI. This was all months prior, 900 SPD personnel, herded into the old Sand Point military facility for the grand re-hearsal with simulated scenarios. A Lakota Sioux was amongst them, a descendent of Sitting Bull, three years into being a Seattle cop. The tribe was very proud of him back at Pine Ridge Rez in the Dakotas near the Black Hills of the Paha Sapa. Was there a psychic conflict? He didn't think so… was it going to be the Battle of Little Bighorn or Custer's Last Stand? Or was it to be Wounded Knee?... Wounded Knee 1890? Or Wounded Knee 1973? Is it all real? To the heart of everything that is...

He appreciated the training and they all liked the new equipment — that all-black hard gear from shin guards to ballistic helmets making them all look somewhere between Darth Vader goon squad to teenage mutant ninja turtles. The Mayor Schell and Police Chief Stamper were all confident that things were covered and it would be just another boon to the Emerald City with 8,000 delegates (note: some of these delegates had played doctors on TV), Clinton showing up, Kissinger and Albright arriving to give speeches, hundreds of international media, all to showcase this star chamber with its spanky opulence as home to Microsoft, Boeing, Starbucks, Trimsetter and REI. The Indians thought the chiefs seemed so sure like it was all gonna land like a big ol jet airliner — smooth onto Boeing Field, a 747 jumbo with pretty stewardesses from Pan-Am, and take off like a supersonic with a deafening whisper. But as indicated, many of the frontline platoons were not so sure. Some were vocal that it was going to be Chicago '68, an ode to Mayor Daly's police riot and a gas, gas, gas... particularly with the pepper spray which is nasty (oleoresin capsicum). Very popular with police departments; part of their arsenal of "safe" weapons. There's only been a hundred or so fatalities in the U.S. and Canada from its use; people going into anaphylactic shock or suffocation after being sprayed tackled and cuffed. Probably not to be considered torture — just another damn accident in the defense of our freedoms. Despite a few deaths, there's no federal or state agency that regulates the manufacture or use of the chemical. No science — what effects the toxin has on human health is an unknown known unknown.

In Seattle the cops were using a 10 percent solution carted around in containers that looked like mini-fire extinguishers. It was MK-46 First Defense Red Pepper manufactured by Defense Technologies (Def-Tech) in Casper, Wyoming. It is made from the extracts of capsicum peppers mixed with an alcohol solution that causes intense burning of the skin, nose, mouth and eyes. Def-Tech, the rap group, cautions that the toxin is meant only to be used for defense purposes in order to protect the safety of the police and should not be sprayed on folks protesting at a distance of less than three feet. And so like a book, there is nothing like directions to confuse one — so it was with some of the union members of the SPD — was it three feet or 3 inches? — as they gratuitously sprayed the stinging solution directly into the faces of the demonstrators, malcontents, performance artists and recreational rioters. But either way, now, training day was upon us against the lead-gray sky, moody — the portent loomed over the city like the blue hump of Mt. Rainier.

Posse Comitatus Act: Passed in the wake of the Civil War specifically placed to bar the federal military from intervening in local police matters.* It was in response to President Grant's post-Civil War effort to use troops to guard ballot boxes and prevent election fraud, Congress had ordered that such police powers rest only at the county level. Federal troops were not allowed from enforcing domestic laws. The legal doctrine of the Posse Act is considered an epitome of American democracy, keeping Presidents from sending soldiers, banana republic style, to impose policy or enforce domestic laws. Some of Nixon's top aides wanted to use troops to round-up left-wing protesters, but J. Edgar informed Commander in Chief that such a move would violate the Posse Comitatus Act. Like to give a shout out to J. Edgar!

This is why it is up to state governors to call up the National Guard to quell civil disorder or cope with natural catastrophes

---

* exceptions have occurred: up to 20,000 regular Army and Airborne troops were sent to patrol the streets of D.C. after the riots broke out with the assassination of Martin Luther King, but… District of Columbia is not a state. Mac was there during the riots, right in the middle of it, at an insane asylum called St Elizabeth's — protecting/guarding all the pretty white college nurses in Anacostia, one of D.C.'s toughest neighborhoods. It was the first Federally operated psychiatric hospital. Mac wound up there with the 101st. Got to do some dancing… definitely an Italian Gothic experience. Months later he attended the nurse's graduation. Ironically, or not ironically, that is the question… the mental institution; St Elizabeth's Hospital, would become the future site for the headquarters of the U.S. Department of Homeland Security.

instead of asking for assistance from the active military. One can see the inherent conflict. This is the continuum of the debate on state's rights versus the federal. It was also part of the opening for Jim Crow Laws… and loitering laws to fill up the chain gangs. That free labor be money. Down South.

Tuesday N/30 or Sweet Home Alabama: soon Seattle would be under civic emergency. None dare call it martial law, but the martial-marshal had come to town and Sharia don't like it, with National Guard choppers hovering over downtown, sweeping the city with searchlights. By 7pm a curfew had been imposed on the crisis party. But thousands said — Forget about it — Vaffanculo!… (we all know what that means) how about some Posse Comitatus? (but we don't know what this means cuz it's in Latin — could even mean: the mob is Rome)… But back in the saddle — these were the same thousands who captured the streets that day; sustained clouds of tear gas, volleys of rubber bullets, concussion grenades and straight-up beatings from riot batons — the street warriors, many of whom were women. Pushing the flaming dumpsters and pallets out onto the pavement along the Old Squid Row, the phalanx set up the barricades — to hold the streets and ultimately — to draw the line as they were pushed up to city's most ravenous district — Capitol Hill — to the corridor of Pike and Pine; they clashed with the Black and Tan forces-for-hire WTO/SPD in front of Irish punk-rock bar Kincora. Drama achieved; everything amok. The menacing flash grenades kept exploding above people's head or whipping around on the ground like sparking loose electrical deadly hissing snakes, all kinds of M-80 like explosions continued as the CS gas floated, hovered burning the eyes. So in the dark of the night, some beatnik from his apartment window with one helluva PA system was playing in high fidelity Aerosmith's "Draw the Line"… Way loud… 'Checkmate honey, beat you at your own damn game No dice honey, I'm livin on a astral plane Feet's on the ground and your head's goin down the drain Oh, head's I win, tails you lose, to the never mind When to draw the line A Indian summer, Carrie was all over the floor She was a wet net winner, and rarely ever left the store She'd sing and dance all night, and wrong all the right outa me Oh, pass the vile and cross your fingers, it don't take time Nowhere to draw the line Hi ho silver, we're singin' all your cowboy songs Oh, you told me Carrie, and promised her you wouldn't be long Heads I win, tails you lose, lord it's such a crime No dice honey, you the salt, you're the queen of the brine… Checkmate honey, you're the only one who's got to choose When to draw the line Checkmate, don't be late Take another pull That's right impossible When you got to be yourself You're the boss of the toss The dice, the price Grab yourself a slice Know when to draw the line…' Walter thought it was all far-fucking out. You use to be able to get any kind of drug you wanted or needed back in the day, twenty cats be comin out of the woodwork and brick and mortar, but not tonight. The street warriors bravery triumphed in stated objective of direct action strategists to hold the line long enough to force the WTO to cancel their big opening day. And they attained it! Balls to you Big Daddy!

On the other side of the thin blue line, the young Lakota cop, exhausted and pissed turned to one of his brothers, a young black cop not much out of academy himself like the Sioux; he is also exhausted and pissed — the Indian says to him, "Things have not been thought through." Somewhere he hears the Garryowen and thinks, what the fuck? Is it his mind? And then he has this vision of an eagle soaring high overhead, screeching… the Wakan Tanka spoke; Crow Dog blesses… and then he knew his days of being a cop were not long. At the same time, over at the Kincora the two owners stood and kept a steely guard — the Samoan NFL football star turns to his partner Boru and says, "Things have not been thought through." From the corner of his eye, Walter caught a glimpse of Andre casually drinking inside the Kincora; probably a nice smooth shot of Jameson. That's perfect Andre — immune, just an observer, taking it all in, drinking it all in… Something about this incensed Walter and it made him push harder; he continued running wild in the streets that evening amongst the smoke and the haze, the cacophony of noise, his sore eyes and the darkness of the night — evading the police, but picked up by one patrol in Black Maria. Just as the storm troopers were upon him a couple of black-garbed ninjas came swooping down upon the scene, tossing a few lit canisters of tear gas back at the cops with one of the ninjas in billy goat gruff voice yelling, "Run Walter!" And he did, as the police pursued the greater offenders, but he did take a second rubber bullet in the back on that one. He knows the three ninjas were Mac, Cat and probably Kamau. He worried about Señor Agape's heart condition as he ran through the streets — all through the night. The plastic bullets hurt real good. He held one in his hand and showed it to some hard-working tax-paying residents of Capitol Hill who were just getting off work and amazed at the gaseous violent melee that had transformed in their quaint hip neighborhood. Anybody on the streets that night by then was open season for being considered an anarcho-trasher and liable to be sprayed or beaten. By then, in there fatigue and frustration, the cops were taking mental shortcuts — even the Christmas carolers — had become collateral damage. Walter got water from them in gallon jugs and got back to the fray to soothe the thirsty, wash the burning eyes of the afflicted and offer succor to the wounded like he had been doing — all through the day. It had been a busy day — abetting protest yet stopping the bigger bombs of Maurice and Mac from being so readily available and going off, stopping assassination attempts or kidnappings of politicos, assisting Bill in the wresting of guns from apoplectic delegates ready to shoot their way into the convention and; avoiding being killed by Louis Willy and Myron X. Thus exhilarated, he continued running thru the streets of Seattle and its underground passageways like Jean Valjean amongst les miserables, the pariahs, the Jacobites and the raparees. He missed his woman.

Walter and Jane had finally consummated their relationship back at Walter's crib. Between the second-hand tradeshow partition walls, pallets and old hanging lilting Hindoo bed sheets, Walter had fabbed up some palatial digs. It was sweet and succulent like apricots in the morning. She was a mammal! He was a mammal! She felt like a woman. He felt like a man. Because the night... belongs to lovers... It was animale and spiritual. Primordial, biological, Evolutionary! present. She almost didn't believe. Jane had gone dyke after her "service" in the military. She had joined the army right after high school — gone Airborne. Wound up in the Persian Gulf War and found all her training and abilities being foisted into serving as a rape counselor for her own sisters in the military. She was kept very busy at this job. This was in Saudi Arabia, our stable ally. After that she was in the Peace Corps for the two years in a little country called El Salvador, did some boat time with Greenpeace, lived in a tree for a year in Oregon, worked for Nader's WAPIRG and clerical temp outfits. That's how she wound up at Trimsetter Corporation and meeting Walter. But first, she had a little talk with Walter: "The problem is you men spend so much of your energy in objectifying behavior whether in business, politics, or sex — often you just end up objectifying yourselves like you're machines as you begin using your own bodies as disposable objects in the pursuit of orgasms, money, or power. I saw a lot of this in the army — it's easy for you bastards — this self-directed objectification because you do it all the time, you're accustomed to treating everything in your environment as a disposable object. You see Walter, it becomes habitual at first — this objectifying process, then compulsive and finally obstructive to all demands from the outside world for respect and reverence. Bingo! You get it? It's an addiction like any drug/alcohol addiction; adrenalin seeking, ego-building rush for the objectifier. Objectifying behavior, when it's compulsive, leads to annihilation of the user, for they burn out their own bodies and psychic emotional energy sources like Roman candles, just as they consume those around them. So you see Walter, all those John Wayne movies — this conditioning of the male for patriarchy, particularly this curious American brand of what it is to be a Man, this unquenchable quest to increase the pleasure, money and power for one's ego — only leads to destroying it! A guy named Evans wrote all about it." Walter, the paramour, listened and then he kissed her, thus they began working on overcoming their terror of intimacy — and they sought, they found… their satellite of love and the God of Ecstasy. Striking a fine perfect balance with the beauty of beast-mode. A real nice high — really the best momentous thing in life. This ring of fire. Simple, and to be conscious and grateful for that. That's where they got that night and to the dawn… She really worked him over good. Last kiss…

The next morning, Jane was leaving back for Wisconsin to help her ailing folks back on the farm, her mother had been stricken with a stroke. She was going to miss the whole shebang protest and she had been deep in it. Working with Ruckus. Jane was heartbroken, but this was a bad emergency and she knew that there would be plenty of protest to come — maybe even in Madison. Walter was somewhat relieved — he didn't really want Jane, his suffragette, his Jezebel to be out there bomb throwing. He missed his woman; like Jesse James, she stole his heart — of what was everything…

Cops were going 24/7 observing the demonstrators who by 5:30am a large group had formed at Victor Steinbrueck Park just north of the Pike Place Market. Mixed in with the crowd besides Señor Agape as penguin, were some very prepared people with gas masks, amongst the steelworkers, sea turtles, Earthfirst!ers, hundreds of signs and giant puppets; a Mardi Gras-like atmosphere with chanting, drums and trombone players. Strangely absent were Mac and Maurice, Walter thought — just MIA. At 7:30, large groups started walking to the convention center from five different locations. By roughly 8 o'clock, seven distinct large-scale disturbances erupted within a radius of a couple of blocks. Sometime after nine, the use of chemical irritants was authorized and very soon after the gas was loosened on the streets, calls for mutual aid came in as ten King County Sheriff's deputies were holding off over a hundred protesters trying to penetrate the underground parking at the Sheraton. While a few blocks away, Bill the Sculptor with other protesters were blocking the entrance to the Paramount where the opening ceremonies were scheduled. That's when a frustrated WTO delegate pulled a revolver from his coat pocket and aimed it at the protesters. Señor Agape, Walter and Bill the Sculptor saw the man with the gun and grappled with him, the police rush in with their billy clubs jabbing the protesters away from the pistol wielding delegate who was neither arrested, detained or stripped of his weapon. He was safely ushered away. Walter had fallen to his knees, he looks up at the rooftop of the Camlin Hotel wondering if Baby Nambu is up there, and he catches a brief glimpse of a figure in VC black that has got to be him, he then looks across the street and sees Maurice in a fine silk Tommy Bahama shirt surreptitiously speaking into a wire oblivious to the chill. A rap hip-hop group with an extraordinary PA system saunters down into the hurly-burly with a catchy tune called "TKO the WTO" — Human chains were formed at the 7th and Pine intersection with the purpose to keep WTO delegates from realizing their morning meetings. Some delegates did not pull guns, but just punched protesters instead. One very hung-over British delegate who had just left the Roosevelt Hotel hit at least two protesters for good measure; in fear of lex talionis, he ran down the street crazed and still quite delirious from the partying the night before at Ziggy Jaeger's Trimsetter billionaire bash extravaganza to beat all the billionaires throwing parties on the other side of the pond at the tony neighborhoods of Carillion Point, Bellevue, Bonnie & Clyde Hill, and Medina… the high-tech nouveau riche of the Seattle Metro area — the new world order of it really. But that poor British delegate was running for his life in his altered state, drunk and pissed off gibbering to himself: "Man, America… where the cocaine proves the purest rock man groove." Somebody finally dragged him into a bar.

By 10 o'clock there was shit breaking out everywhere. As the dragoons were put on alert, squads of riot cops showed up at 6th and Union hollering, "Fifteen minutes warning!" With more cops clinging to the side of the "peacekeeper" vehicles and dozens of tear gas canisters getting unloaded the air began oozing a gray-green smoke. Louis Willy was just wandering out after crashing down under the Alaskan Viaduct, heading for 4th and Yesler, looking for Walter Curmudgeon. He came across some official WTO brochures with something written about "liberalizing" trade policies — "damn liberals" — he thought. What the hell is goin on — leave Detroit, looks like a bombed-out mess with as much shootin goin on as Beirut and here now I'm in Seattle and riots breaking out, subversives in black rags and black bandannas wearin across their face like rustlers, breaking windows at McDonald's. They're throwin shit at officers of the law! It's a city under siege and I haven't even had my mornin constitution yet. I ought to just start doin some citizen arrests on some of these bastards. Where the hell did that Adolf Mungu tell me to meet him and what time? Lookin here at this map I believe I'm in the right territory to find my nemesis Curmudgeon — suppose to be habitating somewhere near here. Ain't too far. Damn gas is startin to burn my eyes. Cough, cough — country's goin to hell. Tryin to get thru these here intersection of 6th and University, all these protesters locked arms, cast in concrete, one big knot of humanity. Cops on the bullhorn — guess we call him a field commander, like old Bull Conner. In violation of the law! he keep sayin that. Why don't they just go and pick them up and arrest their sorry asses? I'm about ready to do it myself again. She-eet cops will arrest me here with two pistols in my pocket and one here little .32 against my calf. I got that new .22 Winchester pump stowed under the bridge — pick me off some of these varmints, but there's all these goddam grandmas and children in cute little sea turtle outfits. O my look at some of them big puppet things — kinda cool. This is a gas, gas, gas — cough, cough, cough... my, my muthafuckin sleeper cells of zombies everywhere and these fuckers all in black — just want to break shit. Yeah, yeah, fuck Nike and them fancy Starbuck's coffee shops, but leave McDonald's alone! What they got against Happy Meals? Haul them bastards off to prisoner transportation units! Shit I must be close now. Prefontaine Street — man, away from some of those chemical irritants, what bullshit — its gas, burns good, we dropped it all over Vietnam too. That's how nice it is. Fourth and Yesler. Yep, interestin place, just like how the Illuminati described it. See if I can see that damn-gum Walter who got me hauled off that ship processor in the Aleutians and sent to the booby hatch, but I made my escape and vengeance will be mine.

Louis Willy looks thru the big antiquated storefront windows with the layered heat-distorted glass. Guess they call it Art. That one thing there looks like it should be a boat anchor and some of these paintings just look like slaughterhouse nightmares. New Museum of Hyster-ia and In-Decision, huh? We B Art Gallery, Brave Dog/ Dead Dog Art Works, Manifesto Party Headquarters, Picaro Press. How many names does this place have? But I know I'm at the right place with Manifesto Headquarters — Free Guns and Dope for Life — sounds like my kind of place, maybe they got a little of that LSCrazee... Seems pretty vacant right now. Gonna ring this bell.

Louis Willy keeps ringin the bell. No response. Ringin. No response. Finally some fancy looking dame comes thru the back opening of the space. She is wearing stilettos, fishnet stockings, got a fur coat and bright red lipstick. Louis Willy thinks my, oh my. She opens the door and says, "Hi doll — you kind of cute — in a scruffy way," as she gives him a little rub and tug on his beard. The good-looking broad appears quite drunk, Louis Willy astutely surmises from all his private detective training he got from a subscription to a magazine called "True Detective" that also, once he passed the test, bestowed upon him a license — as a private detective. Yep, she's pretty drunk. But sexy... Could be my lucky day.

She says, "Come on in Sugar."

In the backdrop continues the sirens, explosions, shots, drums and general uproar and pandemonium taking place in downtown Seattle. Louis Willy thinks, oh she's friendly...

"You want a drink Honey?"

"Mam, I'm looking for a Walter Curmudgeon."

"What you want with that bad man for?"

"He done me wrong up in Alaska a few years back."

Heading to the west wing of the gallery area, she goes to a fridge and pulls out a bottle of gin, nearly full.

"I just got this bottle and like from the Rubaiyat of Omar Khayyam I always say — bring out the gin bottle! I brought it straight from the bar, you know, The 611? they're just down the hill..." she says so innocently with inquiring eyes like Betty Davis eyes. Louis takes the drink she hands him. It's a goblet with some ice and lime and a lot of gin. And he thinks there's somethin funny about her and it isn't just cuz she's drunk. They keep a drinkin and a talkin, sittin down on one of the more comfortable couches.

"Interestin place here." As the parrots fly back and forth, the cats purr, the dog snores and the koi pray silently. More gin is poured. Louis is getting all floaty... momentarily forgettin about Walter, forgettin about meeting up with Adolf Mungu and is just about to kiss the pretty perfumed lady when out from some curtains pops a couple black-garbed ninjas and men in general Mad Max crazed vet/biker pirate attire.

Mac exclaims loudly, "What the fuck have we here? Cat-O-Nine get a load of this — whose this Appalachian victim you got here; you up to that down-low again Myron? In da gay ghetto, damn man... you with all them confused brothers and violent village people types down at the 611 — ain't gay, they just be doin the down-low... What you think?"

Kamau just start laughing with big flashing white teeth like joyous donkey and says, "Yeah that be massively gay a ha-ha-ha like Elton John gay."

"I don't think this po'buckra knows nothin," interlopes Cat without a smile.

"He says he's lookin for Walter — done him wrong," Myron pipes in.

"We're lookin for him too — got a few questions of our own."

Louis Willy, suddenly, with the lucidity that comes thru clear spirits realizes that this beautiful woman with her hand on his thigh, has an Adam's apple, big hands, a 9 o'clock shadow and is getting called Myron. "Hey what the fuck you trying to pull here — you one of them he-shes!?" Louis Willy goes to grab his snub-nosed Smith and Wesson .38 Special revolver "Victory" Model. Cat-O-Nine of Special Forces, immediately relieves Louis Willy of his duties of having a pistol in his hand.

Mac like Omar Khayyam fills the little dinted tin cup with some more of that gin. "Relax we're all friends here." Louis shakes his wrist and elects to keep drinkin.

Then Maurice bursts in from behind some bamboo screens. His fine silk Tommy Bahama shirt is wet with sweat, his eyes are of a wild blue fire, his tanned face has reddened. "Och!" he howls. Mac, Cat and Kamau look with intense curiosity.

"Och!" he howls again, "Le mission est foutu! No Hank! — Like fucking Coup d'Etat! Kissinger is bagging, he's not coming. Fucking Mr. Switzerland is getting a pedicure and his back rubbed with a loofa in Geneva. My sources just got this to me. We've got to get Nambu off the roof. It's breaking apart out there nice. Where's the fucking Molotovs!?" exasperates an apoplectic Maurice. "They're delaying Clinton. Delta Force is on high alert. They'll be calling out the National Guard soon. They've completely lost control. Those direct action folks from Ruckus and the like had their game down. It's all coming together — a State of Emergency; the SPD's Insecurity Plan is working perfectly… a police riot — drama… where's those damn Molotovs? What the fuck is this fruit doing in a dress? And whose the little hillbilly palooka next to him with the bad Castro beard?"

"It's Myron X! and his new boyfriend from Gold Bar or Sedro Wooley or somewhere like that…"

"From dem snake-handlin Hills of Deliverance…"

Maurice just shakes his head and glares momentarily at Myron X, "I always thought he was kind of creepily effeminate. What'd you see goin on out there?"

"We just got here ourselves momentarily lost in the underground. We just left 5th and Pine — to see how our dear Eugene anarchist friends from the Black Bloc are doing? A fine work of mayhem — regular revolt. A Clash." Mac replies.

"Bien, bien Inch'Allah."

"They all be doin just fine," interjected Cat, "with a little help from the street gangs — NWA Ramone be runnin them Crips, he be a shooter if we ever need that. The kids be hopin' it all comes back next year."

"Pilgrim, how can we get Nambu off the roof? Somebody tipped them off." Pilgrim was aka Cat-O-Nine — Maurice knew him by that nom de guerre from back in the halcyon days of the Pheonix Program ridin shotgun with elephants through the Cambodian jungle along the Ho Chi Minh Trail — the horror, the glory, the horror, the glory… "Damn where is Robespierre, the Terror, Thermidor and the guillotine when you need it?! Bring out the trebuchet! We will give them Greek Fire!"

"The trebuchet is down; the big wooden arm is cracked and Jacque and Walker haven't repaired it yet," Mac ses with a sigh of relief.

"Now, now we mustn't upset the Christmas shoppers. Team America — Fuck Yeah!" adds Kamau.

"I could make some calls to Fort Lewis, see if we could get a chopper and get some Delta to fast rope and whisk him away so fast hardly anyone would notice with all the mayhem going on out there now in the streets."

"Yeah I like that idea beaucoup — I don't want to risk Baby Nambu getting pick up coming down the building and out into the streets."

"What do we do with these two?" Mac inquires.

"Let's put them on the roof."

"Yeah, they look pretty guilty to me..."

"What about the Molotov cocktails!?"

"Uh... we were told that Walter had an accident with the old Hyster forklift and crushed all the pallets of Molotovs and destroyed half the pot crop. I really believe it must have been an accident cuz that hophead would never destroy all them beautiful marijuana plants... brings tears to my eyes and it's not the SPD gas. Walter is in deep kimchi."

"What?! No Kissinger! no Molotovs! — we should have mined the harbor!"

"Bottle rockets!" shouts Louis Willy.

"Yeah no Molotovs, but we got bottle rockets." ses Mac.

"I think that Walter's clumsy enough — I think he really might have lost control of the forklift and accidently fucked everything up. He's one dumb mzungu." Kamau interjects.

"The man just don' grasp the facts — he don' ever learn — God just don't save the stupid," ses Cat.

Maurice goes on, "I still want to kill him. If I had my Gurkha kukri — he would not only be Walter Without Belongings; he would be Walter Without a Head."

Mac interjects, "We've sent Nitro out looking for him and Agape. Some of the Revolutionary Communist Party members that were not too stoned said it was actually Señor Agape running amok in the forklift — which does seem more likely. I mean the guy's running around wearing a penguin suit, or maybe that purple Kool-Aid dye Walter applied on that Mohawk he just gave himself — could have twisted him. It's all Inch'Allah," says Mac.

Louis Willy is jibbering incoherently by now chockful of gin and desperately needing some Thorazine while Myron X adjust his wig.

"Hoffa must be getting close to finishing his speech over at the Space Needle and the labor legions in the tens of thousands will be marching soon — they are suppose to join up," adds Cat.

"We can get these guys over to the Camlin much quicker thru the underground," Mac declares.

Cat is making a call to Fort Lewis.

Maurice exhorts, "I got a plan! Frisk them first; get the bandoliers, grab the Mannlicher-Carcano 6.5mm! More gin!"

"Vengeance will be mine!" Louis Willy shouts.

"What's he talking about?"

"He's after Walter Curmudgeon — wants to kill him."

"Perfect."

"Chopper is on its way."

"Copy that."

"Zulu-Tango-Bravo…"

"Shoot the fruit up; give the cracker another cup of gin." Myron X takes out compact and re-applies his lipstick.

"Anybody ever tell you — you look like Charles Bronson." Louis Willy garbles to Mac as he pours him some more gin. Mac then goes to get the bandoliers and the carbine. Cat shoots Myron X up. Maurice goes and gets a Polaroid camera nearby (the gallery party camera for the raves and hip-hop shows) — Mac knows what's up. He returns, gets them to stand up, frisks them and begins adorning Louis Willy with the bandoliers across his scrawny, chicken-bone chest. They get Louis Willy to do his best poses with the guns sans bullets; sometimes sitting or standing next to Myron X who was photographed also with a few pistols in his big hands we know you're the one: pretty little red dress on, fish net stockings and stilettos. Myron X is beginning to fawn over Louis Willy like a spaniel again. They make a handsome couple. Maurice left a few here at the Manifesto Headquarters, put a few of the pics upon their person, and took a few for his own necessity as he would deem fit — get a few to the newspapers or certain government agencies.

"Blackhawk will be there in 27 minutes to extract Baby Nambu," says Cat.

"Tell Nambu to leave the rifle. And get a hold of Hamid."

"Rodger that."

"I'm going out on the streets to see how it's going. You take our patseys via the Seattle Underground to the hotel. Get them on the roof. I'll make some calls. Got to call Adolf and tell him it's off. This might even fuck up Clinton's plans more and they are already on their way to being well fucked up."

"Adolf!" Louis shouts out from his stupor.

"Back to Kicksville men! Put some of that SERE training to work with a little baraka." ses Mac.

"Oui — baraka, with luck — we'll all meet tomorrow mid-morning in Georgetown at Jules Maes Saloon. On Nebraska Street — just down from the Rainier Brewery. We've got a flight out early afternoon. Boeing Airfield. Bon chance. Have fun — and remember: everything in war is simple, but the simplest thing is difficult — Von Clauswitz."

"Inch'Allah."

"10-4."

"Mektoub baby... that which is written must happen..."

"Xin loi mutherfuckers."

"Merde."

"All through the day and all through the night."

Thus the freelance security consultants went on their merry way — for the good of the country. As patriots, it was, God Save the Queen...

Meanwhile, Nitro, with his rich criminal history, patrols the streets of Seattle on a mission to find Walter and bring him in — he destroyed all the Molotovs, but mostly he fucked up a lot of good weed and that really pisses off Nitro. What the fuck are all these people protesting about in the streets? It's just annoying. He heads into a Starbuck's to get a triple caramel latte with sprinkles and they fuck it up and they won't give him back his money; they forgot the fuckin sprinkles! So he walks out and smashes one of the windows. That smashing of the Starbuck's window by Nitro inspired others out on the street to follow suit and like a chain reaction — breakage occurred. Nitro gruffly notices this, thought it was weird, shrugs and walks on down the street. Some little pot-belly cop in riot gear, witnessing the window smashing, jumps in front of Nitro, yells at him and begins to take a swing with his billy club, but before sluggo could make contact Nitro just decks him and the cop finds himself seeing stars and bouncing on his soft ass on to the hard sidewalk. A gas canister falls in front of Nitro, he picks it up and hurls it back at the entourage of police. Nitro's not a big fan of the police. He looks around him as he is surrounded by all these demonstrators, looks over at the police again and ses to himself — these people are crazy — Fuckin cop just about made me spill my coffee. I'm getting the fuck out of here; get in my microbus, drop some L, listen to the Dead and head to the ocean… (and drag a dead skate around on the beach) — And that's what he did.

The chant kept on to a rhythmic beat: "The whole world is watching, the whole world is watching" Bill the Brave Sculptor, Señor Agape, and Walter had migrated over to 6th and Union to sit in with the other demonstrators — waiting for tear gas, just about when the tear gas canisters were fired oozing their gray-green smoke. Walter stood up disoriented and that's when he first got shot by the so-called rubber bullets. It dropped him to his knees. Seeing the young chicks getting shot, provoked a young maddened gallant protester to rush the cops only to get pummeled by the four-foot long clubs and get himself hand-cuffed and dragged across the pavement and hauled off to jail. No more WTO aqui for him. People were now, besides getting gassed to unconsciousness like dazed rabbits, were now also getting shot by the rubber bullets in the knees, face, and groin. These bullets are meant to be fired at areas of the body with large muscle mass like the thighs or the ass. But the cops were already afraid and when fear takes over all the rules of engagement go bye-bye; so that over the next two days, Seattle cops would fire off thousands of rounds with no bars hold — it was a free fire zone. By the end of it, the cops weren't only fearful — they were exhausted. They had not been getting water to hydrate themselves in all that infernal gear. No piss breaks. No relief breaks. The plans for this — if there were any to begin with; fell woefully short of being adequate. Might have been too much SWAT training, not enough on logistics and supply — the unsexy stuff. They were just overwhelmed by the sheer numbers and that's when the cops really started getting some shit thrown at them. They had no control, thus the whole situation began to spiral out of control. More volleys of tear gas were not the solution. The fumes overtook the downtown district, the burning dumpsters began to roll and the glass began to break. Walter and Señor Agape both took a couple of quick whacks to their sides from the riot clubs — it was hard to see thru the fumes. Meanwhile, Bill the Sculptor was being assaulted by very upset Christmas shoppers who were hitting him due to the buying interruption with their bags and boxes, but at least none of them pulled out a gun. Walter observed him doing some kind of spinning Estonian dance of sorts with them almost in merriment. Walter caught a glimpse of Andre on the sidewalk running around with a camera and large lens taking photos of the general fracas — and then suddenly he disappears into the haze like an apparition.

Walter staggers over to where he last spotted him. His eyes stinging, his lips burning; Walter was having a hard time breathing. He stumbles by a few storm-troopers. He thought it was a good day to die, but it was like he was invisible and they let him pass right through them. As the sweat pours, he wanders up an alley, his vision blurred, a gentle hand took his and softly said, "Here let me wash your eyes so that you may see…"

"Who are you?"

"I am Star." The coolness of the water was immediate relief and within seconds Walter could see again, but all he saw of the gentle hand was a figure in black garb, long brown hair and a gas mask turn the corner and back into the fray. And she was gone. Farewell, my lovely… Walter then knew what his mission was going to be — all through the day and all through the night. Carry water. And the battle continued and back into it he went, finding Señor Agape holding, locking hands, getting pepper sprayed, having tear gas canisters dropped upon them and being pounced upon by baton wielding police. Dozens of protesters were knocked unconscious. Walter and Señor Agape helped the bloodied and bruised. Bill smiled with his gimlet eyes, it was 2 in the afternoon. The cops backed off. The 6th and University Street intersection had been held. All through the day, it would go — all through the night.

Note: There had been a lull in the action for a couple of hours in the tear gas assaults. Out on the streets no one could explain — the cops had run out of gas… and had to send out a supply plane to Montana to pick up 3,300 pounds of more toxic CN gas. And with that the most liberal city banned the sale, purchase and possession of gas masks. Another note: We need air to breathe…

Walter, Bill and Señor Agape wound up back at the Washington State Convention Center, making their way through all the tumult and eventually back at the Paramount Theatre. Walter again stared up towards the roof of the Camlin Hotel looking for Baby Nambu to see if he was still up there. As far as Walter knew Henry Kissinger was still scheduled to arrive. And Walter to his amazement watches a chopper arise from nowhere, drop a line and pluck what had to be Baby Nambu right from the roof of the old hotel. It was a slick pick as other choppers circled. Swirling with the choppers Walter saw the flying monkeys. It was Oz. He glanced around almost desperately to see if anyone else had noticed what he just witnessed, but with all the noise, smoke and confusion, nobody else was looking up at the sky, it seemed, but he alone. The fog of war. And then to his utter amazement, he sees Louis Willy and what looks like a prostitute in a red dress on the roof of the Camlin. He blinks twice and cleans his glasses. It can't be. The prostitute displays a remarkable resemblance to Myron X. All of the sudden, Walter becomes aware that Louis Willy and Myron X see him as well. He's in kind of the middle of a sit-in/stand-in and he notices a couple of little puffs of concrete dust popping at his feet and Señor Agape's. He then notices a few puffs hitting the cementious columns above their heads. And he glares up at the rooftop of the Camlin and views what could only be described as a hillbilly version of a scene from "The Day of the Jackal" as Louis Willy is up there with a sniper rifle and silencer plinking at them. Walter immediately pounces on Señor Agape knocking him to the ground as well as pushing Bill down in the process just as a bullet hits the ticket stand with a poof right behind where Señor Agape had just been standing. It would have been a show-stopper heart shot. Señor Agape is most annoyed, but Bill is just use to it by now. And right after that last shot by Louis Willy a dozen SWAT team, U.S. Marshalls and F.B.I. agents burst through the rooftop door of the Camlin and apprehend Louis Willy and Myron X for conspiracy to assassination. A few people looked up and became aware of some kind of scuffle up on top of the Camlin, but that was the extent of it. It didn't go public. There was already enough bad press and general embarrassment. The Feds didn't want it known that there was a conspiracy of assassination on Kissinger or some other high government official that was close enough to a reality that there was an actual shooter on a roof. The delay of Clinton's arrival and the boiling squawking of Secretary of State Madeline Albright stuck in her hotel suite was beyond humiliating to the powers that be. The cover-up was complete. It became just a vague rumor. The mayor and the police chief were never informed of it. It was not in the official report. And nothing on the flying monkeys either. Thus, Louis Willy and Myron X became the first detainees to wind up in various Eastern European black sites till they eventually find themselves at Guantanamo. Waiting for the Taliban.

An injury to one is an injury to all: the crackdown would occur that night and carry into Wednesday. The thousands of street warriors wound up waiting for the legions of labor? The thirty thousand that were suppose to march and reinforce them never arrived — like stuck on the beach, Bay of Pigs — waiting for air cover. Some deal was brokered with Hoffa/Sweeny and Clinton/Gore to garner a seat at the table as Hoffa/Sweeny like to put it. Some of the more militant unions had members join in the melee, a phalanx of the IBEW, the Steelworkers and the Longshoremen, disavowing the herders, but they were the minority. Nonetheless, the opening ceremonies of the WTO ministerial had been cancelled. The siege tower had a Seattle police SWAT teams converge on the contraption inadvertently working as a diversion to allow the direct action groups to secure positions encircling the convention center, the nearby hotels and WTO venues.

It got so bad the city officials made a request to the Seattle Fire Department to implement their fire hoses to quell the revolt. The Seattle Fire Department to their credit refused. That a request like this was made was also never made public. Just another rumor like a rumor of war.

Walter and Señor Agape eventually wound up staying at the Kalakala with Bill the Brave Sculptor and night watchman. Wednesday promised to be another busy day.

To foreshadow, it got so bad Wednesday that Dick's Drive-in, the icon of a Seattle hamburger stand, closed at 6pm on Broadway in Capitol Hill. No cheeseburgers… no Pepsi; the aftermath of War. Not too far from Dick's on Broadway at 7am, a consortium collected itself at Seattle Central Community College on and began to march toward downtown. They were immediately confronted by a line of riot police in their surreal Darth Vader-like costumes on 6th Avenue. It had become apparent that today is not going to be a day of suppressing civil disobedience, looting, or rioting. No it was about keeping the rabble in line and stopping political speech. The Clampdown had occurred and many cops are now carrying AR-15s — and them don't shoot no rubber bullets. The heart of the city, the downtown, was a "no protest zone" with entry controlled by the police and National Guard. Exceptions were made for Christmas shoppers, WTO delegates, business owners and workers, residents and emergency and security personnel. This clampdown was a serious violation of the US Constitution — just a little reminder for all us citizens — we really only have the rights we can defend. The mayor, in his creation of a police-state, went against a US Supreme Court case called Collins vs. Jordan which dictates that city governments are compelled to allow protests to happen close enough so that they can be heard and seen by the intended audience. By this closure, like a vanishing trick, Mayor Shell committed a stark violation of the law; but at least we were safe and shoppers could shop. It went further, pushed by the Clinton regime's security apparatus, Seattle officials were not just suppose to have the police suppress riots or looting, but were told to stop dissent of any visible form — against the WTO, from pamphleteering to even holding signs. Call it a harsh censorship of political speech. By 10 am that Wednesday, a guy on 6th Avenue was body-slammed by a goon squad of cops for passing out copies of a New York Times story from that morning on the rampages of the police tactics from the day before. Another protester/pamphleteer had the gall to be handing out copies of the Bill of Rights — his politically incorrect papers were confiscated by the gun-slinging authorities. Walter, Bill and Señor Agape had grabbed a few off the sidewalk and they were immediately absconded off with and they were told to, "move along, move along…" as dozens from the National Lawyer's Guild ran about in green t-shirts identifying themselves as legal observers, taking notes on police brutality incidents to record the tales of unwarranted and unprovoked shootings, gassings and beatings. Dozens of protesters were arrested and placed in plastic wrist cuffs and left sitting on the sidewalk for hours after that first encounter of the morning at 6th Avenue between the police and the protesters. More than were arrested all day on Tuesday. Señor Agape was out of his penguin outfit and was wearing more of a purplish Rashneeshee/Hare Krishna outfit. Somehow they managed not to get arrested after that first sortie of Wednesday. Then, like Cossacks, police mounted on horses, began to encircle the marchers at Rainier Square and began targeting the lead organizers of the protesters. Plainclothes cops with photos in their hands ambled about scanning and identifying those to seize and drag off for the police falange as the marchers occupied the intersection at Denny singing, "We Shall Overcome" and Señor Agape, who was hard of hearing from all the rock concerts, began chanting, "Kum Ba Yah" — more surrealism for Walter. Bill thought it was great and started drawing pictures. But with the sophisticated use of cellphones and walkie-talkies the protesters continued to outmaneuver the cops; frustrating the police hierarchy as they later on grappled for excuses. The Counterpunch delivers…

The arrests continue. The marches continue as does the application of blunt-force trauma. One march headed to the Sheraton but was beaten back by the Cossacks on horses. Walter, Bill and Señor Agape decide to make their way past four police barricades and head to the International Media Center. They watch along with many others Bill Clinton on the TV — he is speaking at the Port of Seattle. He denounces Tuesday's violence. But encourages the WTO delegates to listen to the views of the legitimate protesters — even though he doesn't much agree with most of them, though he believes some of them should be allowed to observe the proceedings. Then Bill met with some of the more compliant heads of the environmental groups to discuss logging, the rain forests, agriculture practices and safe food; gave 'em some hugs and kisses — and said: "What about the children?" — grins, and describes the events outside his suite in the Westin as "a rather interesting hoopla." He expresses his sympathy for the views of those in the streets while his team was ordering with imperious edicts that Seattle Mayor Paul Shell use all available force to clear the streets — for the tourists are money! Bill Clinton — the peacemaker, with his usual masterful panache for sleight-of-hand legerdemain Billspeak, blamed the violent crackdown and violation of the Posse Comitatus Act on the mayor, the Seattle police and the WTO itself, for the chaos and battle that occurred even with the arrival of a contingent of the US military to the scene from Special Forces and Delta. Now that's politics…

Bill quit jabbering on the TV and the three musketeers of Walter, Bill the Sculptor, not Bill the President, and Señor Agape, who is wearing a burka in solidarity for the freedom of Afghani women, decide to make their way to the Labor Temple for the afternoon march that the Steelworkers have gotten sanctioned by the mayor to perform a mock "Seattle Steel Party" dumping Styrofoam steel girders from the docks into Elliot Bay. A couple of speeches and they fish the Styrofoam girders out displaying a new-found green conscience. The rally breaks up and hundreds of Steelworkers join the other protesters in an impromptu march down First Avenue. They make it to the Pike Place Market and are greeted by paramilitary riot squads who rock them with a fusillade of Montana CN gas, flash bombs and rubber bullets. This indiscriminate onslaught hit holiday shoppers and the Metro buses. To be even more intimidating, the cops had been doing this goon squad, goose-stepping march, smacking their big billy clubs against their shin-guards making for a very threatening sound — all part of control-addictive technology. It had started Monday, but they had really ratcheted it up that by Wednesday afternoon at the Pike Street Market — it bust loose. Señor Agape turns to Walter and says, "This reminds me of Pinochet's Chile or witnessing Franco's La Guardia — riding double-up on motorcycles with the guy on back shooting from the hip with sawed-off shotguns…" There were more than 20 volleys of tear gas attacks involving hundreds of police. It was to be some of the most violent of the street battles. And Walter kept getting water, picking people up, tossing back the searing hot canisters of gas at the advancing black wall of cops. The concussion grenades were launched above the crowd's heads, exploding and sending people scurrying for cover up alleys, behind dumpsters and into storefronts entrances as the shrapnel flew. Walter, like a Saint Clair, took a young woman with a five year old and covered them to protect them from the gas and pulled them into a store for safety. It was getting mad, mad, mad out there. "That was sweet!" as one Seattle cop was caught on tape exclaiming after one tremendous explosion. Sweet it was… sweet it was… Putting out the fire with gasoline…

This urban assault against a city's own citizens is what is called "asymmetrical warfare" by defense theorists and Seattle had become the proving ground. The Seattle officials claimed they were caught off guard even though there were numerous reports by the New York Times and the Wall Street Journal on the projected organizing for the Seattle protests. There were claims that a city ordinance called the Seattle Police Investigations Ordinance had prohibited them from doing covert work on individuals or groups solely on their political affiliation. This had been passed in 1979 to restrict police powers after it came to light that the Seattle police had amassed thousands of dossiers on people because of their politics. It didn't want the cops spying and infiltrating groups if they weren't breaking the law. The cops should have just taken a look at the web sites of the Ruckus Society. The Emerald City was not looking so shiny what with all the vandalizing of the corporate stores of McDonald's, Starbucks, Niketown, Banana Republic, the Gap, Bank of America and Trimsetter by anarchists wearing Nikes. The independent boutique shops were left alone while a black city councilman with his embossed gold business card identifying him as such was pulled roughly from his car and denied entry to a WTO reception and threatened to be handcuffed. That $400 suit just didn't cut it. But still some of the NGOs, such as Carl Pope of the Sierra Club, bashed the violence of the protests, worrying that it delegitimized the positions of the NGOs while saying nothing of the violent onslaughts by the police, the National Guard and the corporate sweatshops. All apologies like Vichy collaborators, they worried about the eerie Third Reich resembling design logo of the Niketown sign's chrome letters getting tossed to the folks occupying the intersection below, cheering wildly and some banging on kettle drums by Korean farmers and workers, a few dressed in their multicolored traditional garb who had been exploited for decades. Down goes facade! The Rainforest Action Network had got the ball rolling by having some of their activist climb the side of the building across the street and unfurl a huge banner of the rattlesnake from the "Don't Tread on Me" but instead had it read "Don't Trade on Me" — tears had come to Señor Agape's eyes as he witnessed this inspirational symbolism. He had witnessed police crackdowns in Indonesia and Vietnam to protect Nike's factories from worker actions.

By Wednesday night the cops had pushed the protesters back up into Capitol Hill, the densest neighborhood north of San Francisco for some more sub-poppin, mo'rockin riotin! This was well outside the curfew zone and the no protest area. But they came, they saw, hundreds of police; to protect the East Precinct on 12th from being mobbed by this rabble and taken over. The siege: wasn't going to happen. What an imagination. Now this would have been on par with the New York Draft Riots of 1861 and made one helluva movie... but we Americans are a little out of practice of this sort and prefer to export our violence by joining the army, travelling to distant, exotic lands, meeting strange and unusual people, and killing them — for the Empire... O Corruptions of Empire...

They had been running all through the day and all through the night and Bill turns to Walter and Señor Agape and ses, "All this CS gas is making me thirsty, let's go to the Off-Ramp or the Liberty. Maybe Linda's." Señor Agape, the renegade, defrocked dharmic priest agreed — saying, "Some alcohol might help my heart condition — be brave, be kind, be strong dear Walter — namaste," throwing in a little Hindoo Sanskrit. As Walter had not been shot by rubber bullets in the butt enough, nor bludgeoned by billy clubs to a satisfactory level; and he required more CS gas and pepper spray for his eyes to see more, burn more... his ears desired more concussive grenades to disorient to hear more clearly the clarion call. And thus, at that late hour, two of the three musketeers went to drink heavily, leaving Walter on his journey to the end of the night, with the last hundred.

That night, Derdowski, a member of the King County Council heads up to the Capitol Hill District to mediate and finds himself gassed along with thousands of residents just getting off work trying to return to their homes; some of whom wound up getting beaten, kicked, nearly run over by police vans and shot with rubber bullets. They were at the wrong place at the wrong time — they were in their neighborhood. The ACLU and National Lawyer's Guild investigators were kept very busy on the battle-strewn streets of that most honorable night. Walter went to the defense of a waitress just getting off work and trying to get home and wound up getting pushed, frisked and pepper sprayed with blunt-force trauma application. It was nearly a repeat scenario of the Paramount reggae peace show, like Deja-vu; Walter intervenes, gets pummeled severely by several of the jackboots, but this time he gets sprayed in the face with some mace, handcuffed and arrested and like a hallucination he can see it all happening — separating his body from his mind.

THURSDAY: On the bloody morning after…

Walter finds himself in jail with 600 other demonstrators. They have been hauled off to the old Sand Point Naval Base next to Lake Washington. He coughs up a small amount of blood. He is held for 72 hours without being arraigned, allowed medical attention or contact with a lawyer, but there is one attorney amongst the incarcerated, an Esquire Gibson whose business card is the smiling monkey/ Get Out of Jail Free from the game Monopoly. Chance — how apropos… His legal business is with Indians and criminal defense — when he's not in Vegas. He becomes everybody's counsel at the Sand Point jail. The WTO talks collapse. The African nations refuse to give in to US demands. US Trade Rep. Charlene Barshevsky delivers harsh threats, but to no avail. They resist — namaste bitches. The acrid stench of the CS gas pervades and sours the air in the streets of Seattle that morning… if one listened closely 0they could hear echoes of the stun grenades. Somebody, somewhere — out there, begins playing the theme song from The Sopranos by Alabama 3 — "Woke up this morning!…" This really happened.

A thousand or so congregate and a dozen or so beat on drums in solidarity with those hundreds stuck behind bars that Thursday night behind the King County jail. The cops leave them alone and it remains almost an eerily peaceful happening given the context of the last couple of days. And the drum beats on… the moon wavers ever so and there's a howlin wolf…

Chapter Ten

Memory

> Memory is like riding a trail at night with a
> lighted torch. The torch casts its light only so
> far, and beyond that is darkness.
>
> *– Lakota saying*

Clang, clang... go the jail doors. Under lavender skies, Walter is released from King County jail along with a hundreds of others. He is free. Feeling most dejected and yet exhilarated and victorious at the same time; he contemplates the last couple of days, the last couple of weeks, the last couple of months — it was like a mirage. Remember? What could he possibly forget? What was he suppose to remember?... He comes up to the Indian John T. who carves the red cedar, and has seen it all in a 400 year war. This is Indian land... He smiles at Walter, Walter smiles back. Walter makes his way towards the New Museum of Hysteria and Indecision. It's closed. Metro has taken over the space. There is almost no sign of the world and culture that had existed just a few days before — it has vanished like millions of buffalo, castles made of sand, Walter observes, as the Metro workers haul out the grow lights and the pallets and the kerosene and the Rainier beer. Ted Joans is there retrieving some of his books of Beat poetry as he's got some Charlie Parker playing... He tells Walter he is a hero, like an unknown soldier. And nobody knows… He tells him rumor has it Señor Agape is back in India, Maurice and Mac, with their Thompson guns, are headed to Mombasa; Kamau, the Kikuyu, is up in the Pribs crabbing, Hamid's on his way to Algeria, Bill's MIA and Andre and Danger Woman are sailing on a yacht outside of Antibes. Liem has taken all the animals; fish, parrots, cats and all back to his shop in Chinatown 'cept for Godot; Ted will take Godot. The other associates he did not know of… He said Walter could stay at his place and then he says, "Yes Walter, this has been quite the post-modern pastiche, but just remember; jazz is my religion and surrealism is my life, as we seek sublime forgiveness." And he gives him some doe, a little scratch to cover some potatoes — so Walter has twenty dollars in his pocket. Walter thanks him and with like a crown of thorns, walks on down the lane, seeking his sentimental Calvary — heading to Tai Tung's; feeling like a man — defiant — he was hungry.

Walter looks down at the cracked sidewalk as he sees an empty bottle of gin, and he hears a song by Social Distortion coming from an apartment above as he trudges along with his ball and chain.

Hip-hop, hip-hop and it all fades to gray — singin du wap ditty, ditty-dum ditty-dum. Bink! It blinks out, like a black and white TV. Last tango. How it is… how it is… Once upon a time.

About the Author

While C. PARKS is chairman of the Arkansas Federation of Young Republicans and a member of the Republican State Committee of Arkansas, he is also acting treasurer and vice president for the Committee for Salvation. His book will not be popular with some Republicans because it is not a partisan diatribe. The author has a degree in philosophy.

With the proceeds and donations from this book the author hopes to recoup all his losses.